The

CU00866187

T
FACTORY

Written by
MARK WEST

Hersham Horror Books

Mark West

HERSHAM HORROR BOOKS
Logo by Daniel S Boucher

Cover Design by Neil Williams 2016
Copyright 2016 © Hersham Horror Books
Story copyright Mark West 2016
ISBN: 978-1535551625

The Primal Range
First Edition.
First published in 2016

The Factory

Also from
Hersham Horror Books:

Alt-Series

Alt-Dead
Alt-Zombie

PentAnth-Series

Fogbound From 5
Siblings
Anatomy of Death
Demons & Devilry
Dead Water

The Cursed Series

The Curse of the Mummy
The Curse of the Wolf
The Curse of the Ghost
The Curse of the Zombie
The Curse of the Monster
The Curse of the Vampire

Dedication:

For
Alison & Matthew,
as always

THE FACTORY

Chapter 1

The canal towpath was dark and deserted, the only sound the water lapping gently against the sides.

Tom Williams stared at the outline of the Pocock factory, dark against the navy blue of the sky, as he walked towards it. Some of the windows on the upper floors reflected the light of the pale half moon. He'd looked forward to exploring this place for so long that if he were a man given to whistling, Tom would have done so.

He stopped level with the edge of the building, glanced both ways along to towpath to check he was alone and ran up the short concrete slope to the retaining wall. A six-foot fence that encircled the factory - and had, until the past week, been patrolled - was moored here and he quickly shinned over it, dropping carefully to the rough ground inside. Crouching low, he slid off the lightweight backpack and crossing to the building, pressing his back against the brick.

He'd been an urban explorer for a long time and took the activity seriously, adhering to the "take nothing but pictures, leave nothing but footprints" philosophy as often as he could. Sometimes, of course, you had to bend those rules and he would have gladly done so with Pocock's, if it hadn't been for the guards. The building had called to him since he'd first heard the stories, the ones the old boys in the pubs would re-tell if someone bought them a pint or a chaser.

Tom did like a good ghost story.

It was a phone call from his old friend Paul that alerted him. Tom was in Paris, closing a consultancy contract that was rich enough to mean he could take a couple of months off. He'd planned to jet to Miami with a client who had a private suite at the Dolphins Sun Life Stadium - he didn't enjoy American Football too much, but the weather was great and he knew a man who could line up a couple of girls.

"Old Mrs Pocock died last week," Paul had said.

Tom, his attention waning, had muttered something.

"Yeah," Paul said, eager to impart his information, "and her family's put the site on the market."

That peaked his interest. "When?"

"Within a couple of days, the greedy bastards."

"Has it sold yet?"

"No," Paul teased and Tom could almost hear the gloat in his voice. "But the guards have been removed."

"Fuck off."

"Swear to God."

"Shit, that's excellent."

"Did you want to check it out?"

"Of course I do! I could be home within the next few days."

"Did you want to stay over?"

"It's no problem for me to book a hotel."

"I wouldn't hear of it."

"Then that would be fine, thank you."

"Shall I get some kit together?"

"I'll bring mine up, I take it you want in too?"

"Of course, mate."

The last two days in Paris had dragged, his mind wandering. On the way up the M1 from Luton airport, he'd rung Paul to find he'd gone down with a bug and couldn't make the exploration. He made the right noises but was secretly pleased, he wanted to break the buildings cherry on his own. He drove straight into Gaffney, booked into the Hadley Hall hotel, got himself kitted up and went into town.

Paul had replaced the padlock on the main door but only he had the key, which meant Tom had to break in. He'd found a PDF of the plans and printed them out, examining them in detail on the plane so the layout was fresh in his mind. And he'd found the perfect place to infiltrate.

With a final glance at the towpath, he stood up, turned and hit the frosted glass pane in the middle with a small hammer from his backpack. There wasn't a lot of noise but he dropped back into a crouch and waited to see if it attracted any attention, counting to fifty. At fifty-one, he ran the hammer around the frame and knocked out all the glass, put the hammer back in his rucksack and slid the head-torch onto his forehead.

He pulled himself through the window and, as per the plan, found himself in a toilet block. He went out into a small ante-room and through the door of that into a larger room he couldn't see the end of. There were panel windows to his left, on the outside wall, which let in a minimal amount of light. The ceiling was low, with metal beams leading off into the darkness and light fixtures, coated with thick cobwebs that hung down like streamers. There were large pieces of equipment in front of him and, beyond them, long benches. The room smelled strongly of leather and there were stacks of wicker baskets in the corner.

This was the rough-cutting room. He was aiming for the basement, which couldn't be accessed from here - he had to get into reception, through to the maintenance area and down from there.

He took a couple of deep breaths, psyching himself up. It didn't matter how many Urbex's he went on, there was still a similar sensation to each one. A sense of adventure, certainly - and Tom lived for the adrenaline rush - but also the sense of touching history, a shared past that hadn't been looked at or explored for years. He didn't often talk about it, worried that he wouldn't be able to do the sensation justice with words but he felt it.

He made his way across the room, alternating between looking at the floor and looking straight ahead. Old buildings could have rotten floorboards or an outcropping of metal that would end an exploration very quickly and he had to be extra vigilant since he was alone. At the door, he turned right into a narrow corridor and followed that to the reception area.

Someone spoke and he felt a quick jolt of fear. He knew it was probably coming from outside but it was still startling and he held his breath, waiting to hear it again. He didn't, so he crossed the room, sticking as close to the wall as possible to avoid leaving footprints in the dust.

There were two doors on the far wall, one marked 'offices', the other blank. He chose the blank one. He followed a short corridor and passed several offices. Ordinarily he would have systematically worked his way through each one, photographing interesting things, but not today. He followed the corridor through the workshops, which smelled thickly of oil and leather. Windows, high up on the walls, let in a small amount of light. What tools he could see were on mostly filled shadow boards - clearly the guards, dogs and fencing had done a good job.

Ahead, a set of big sliding doors swam out of the gloom, marked "Tanning". He was almost there.

"Where…"

The voice was a whisper, the speaker over his shoulder. He turned quickly, saw he was alone.

"Stupid," he said and kept walking. He'd done this often enough to know the audio tricks an old building could play - a vibration could sound like a voice, settling could sound like footsteps, echoes could take on a life of their own.

"Where are…" the voice came again.

Tom felt a chill in his shoulders and he rolled them, trying to loosen up.

"…you going?"

Tom stopped and turned a full circle, taking in the room as far as he could see it. He prided himself on being a rational man, but knew this wasn't an audio illusion.

"To see you," he called into the darkness, "why else?"

He only heard the faint echo of himself so kept walking, the fear regressing with each step as his confidence grew. Perhaps he was on the right trail then.

James Pocock, who'd had the factory built and ran it until his disappearance at the turn of the previous century, had fascinated Tom after he overheard stories of the industrialists behaviour, both with his workforce - a lot of which was child labour - and his treatment of people. By the time he began his research, Pocock's sister had shut the building up, as if trying to hide something, which Tom spent a lot of time getting to the bottom of.

Tom pulled open the Tanning room door. Metal squealed against metal, initially startling him and he felt a sudden flop sweat on his forehead and top lip. He kept pulling, the door opening gradually, protesting every inch.

The voice was in front of him now. "Where are you going?"

"Coming to find you," Tom said, "down in the basement."

If his research was right, he would discover the old man didn't die a blameless death in his sleep but, instead, never left the factory. That would help to explain some of the ghost stories he'd heard and collected over the years.

The Tanning room appeared to be empty, though there were patches of darkness deeper than others, as if large objects were hanging from the rafters. With the PDF in mind, he walked at an angle thirty-degrees to the doors, checking the floor for damage.

Something moved behind him, a brushing sound that instantly alerted him. It wasn't the building settling, so had someone perhaps seen him come in and followed him?

As he turned, nothing showed in the reach of his torch. The sound came again, to his right and he adjusted his gaze. His heart beat had increased and his mouth felt dry.

The brushing was now spread around him.

"I want my mummy…" said a small voice, almost in front of him.

Tom yelped and stepped backwards. As he did, shapes began to appear out of the gloom, small and lumpy and it took him a moment to realise they were children dressed in ill-fitting clothes.

"Very funny," he said, annoyed with himself. Scared by kids, what a big and brave Urbexer he really was. "Why don't you fuck off out of it?"

"Please help us, mister," said someone to his left and

the shapes moved forward.

He felt a chill again in his shoulders because there was something wrong here. They came towards him quickly and he backed away, trying to match their pace. More movement and now he could hear breathing, raspy as if the person was ill.

"Who are you?"

"We just want you to help, guv'nor."

He stepped back, suddenly afraid. These weren't kids who'd followed him in, he was sure of it. He turned and ran, trying to keep the same angle he'd been on before. A bench seemed to appear from nowhere and he tried to throw himself to one side, avoiding it. His hip connected with the edge, sending a bolt of flame down his leg and across his belly. He grunted in pain as he stumbled sideways, falling onto his back. The kids quickly surrounded him, all talking at once, some of them singing. He lashed out at them but didn't connect once.

"Get away from me!" he screamed, pushing himself backwards. Fear and panic, two things he didn't want to experience, flooded through him, threatening to overtake his senses. He thought he had it all figured out, but hadn't anticipated this in the slightest. His headtorch came off, quickly consumed by the shadows.

Tom got to his feet, his hip flaring with pain and hobbled away as quickly as he could. He couldn't tell where he was in relation to the doors and could barely see anything either, but he could hear snuffling, rasping breath of the children as they matched his pace.

He wished Paul had come, even if just to sit outside in the car, at least someone would have known he was in here.

His breath was a harsh sound, burning in his throat

and chest. He saw a pale shape against the back wall. Could it be a door? He hobbled quicker, the pale shape growing more defined. He saw the handle, held out his arm ready to grab it. Something brushed his and he screamed again but kept moving.

The door was so close as he pushed himself on. Something grabbed his rucksack, trying to tug him back but he shrugged it off. He reached the door, yanked the handle and pushed, rushing through it.

There was nothing on the other side. His right leg was suspended in mid-air and he couldn't figure it out. Instinct kicked in and he looked up, saw the crane arm above the door and grabbed for it as his momentum carried him forwards. Suddenly he was holding himself up, his biceps instantly groaning with the pressure.

His legs swung out and he looked down three storeys to the towpath.

How the fuck had that happened? He'd been on the ground floor, he knew he had.

Tom's fingers slipped on the rough metal and he swung his legs, trying to allow himself to get a better grip. He managed it, but within moments could feel paint flaking under his fingertips. He looked down, his stomach churning. Would he hit the water or concrete?

More paint flaked and his biceps burned. He surely couldn't hold himself up much longer.

Could he swing himself over the water? How deep was the canal here? Even if it was shallow, surely two broken legs would be better than landing on concrete.

A big blister of paint shifted under his left hand, blinding him and allowing his fingers to lose contact with the crane arm altogether. He swung, unable to control his motion or open his eyes. He rubbed them with his left hand and grabbed for the crane arm again. He couldn't reach it.

His fingers slipped until he was barely hanging on.

"No!"

His fingers slid off the metal and he screamed all the way down to the concrete.

Chapter 2

Sunlight found its way through a gap in the curtains and Paul Barrett moved his head away from the glare, his eyes flickering open. It took him a moment to come too and then he felt the ebb of pain in his stomach and throat. The worst was clearly past, but he still groaned, having just suffered a horrible twenty-four hour bug that had laid him out.

His mouth tasted like someone had been standing in it for days. Slowly, he sat up and waited as his head, thick and clogged, settled. His stomach still ached but his shoulders now only felt uncomfortable and not like someone had sprinkled broken glass in the joints. A cup was on the bedside cabinet and he gingerly reached for it, thinking his headache might be dehydration. He took a swig of water and retched - it had gone warm. How long had it been stood there? He licked his cracked lips, took a deep breath and checked his watch. It was after two. He wondered if Tom had tried to get in touch, to tell him about his adventure at Pococks.

Stupid fucking bug, he thought. The first chance he'd had to go exploring with his old college buddy and he'd been laid out, barely able to move. Tom had rung, made sure he was alright but Paul didn't know how long it'd been since then. Maybe he'd left a message?

He pushed himself off the bed carefully and waited until he'd got his balance before moving. The silence of the flat seemed to echo as he made his way across the narrow landing to the bathroom. He went to the toilet, his piss the colour of jonquils, cleaned his teeth and splashed water on his face. Drying off, he stared at himself in the mirror - dark rings circled his eyes, his face looking terribly lined. He made his way to the kitchen and put the kettle on, thinking a good strong cup of coffee would do him good.

His mobile rang and it took him a moment to realise it was in the lounge. By the time he'd got to it, the caller had gone to voicemail and when he picked up the handset he saw half a dozen missed calls from a number he didn't recognise.

"Bloody PPI," he said and went to make his coffee. The phone rang again five minutes later, the same number.

"Hello?"

"Ah, hello," said a female voice he didn't recognise, "is this Paul Barrett?"

"It is and I feel like crap, so I'm not in the mood to buy anything."

There was a pause. "I'm not selling you anything, Paul," the caller said, a hitch in her voice. "My name is Brenda Williams."

"Mrs Williams?" he asked.

"I've been trying to reach you for a while."

"I'm sorry, I haven't been well."

"I have some bad news."

Why would she be ringing to tell him bad news, that didn't make sense at all. "What's happened?"

"It's Tom, he's gone."

He heard the words but they made no sense. "He hasn't gone, he's here in Gaffney."

"No dear," said Brenda Williams with the lightest touch of steel in her voice, "he's gone. We lost him

16

yesterday."

Paul collapsed into a chair. "But I spoke to him yesterday."

Brenda tried to say something else but tears got the better of her, cloaking the words in sobs. He waited for her to calm down, staring out the window at the blue sky and the contrails a plane was leaving. He felt number than yesterday, when Tom rang and asked when they were meeting up.

Finally, with several deep breaths, Brenda had herself under control. "I'm sorry, I thought I'd be able to deal with it. But I know how close you two were and how much you meant to him."

That phrase made his own tears come. "What happened?"

"They don't really know for sure yet, but he was found in the canal early this morning."

"The canal?" That didn't make any sense either.

"I'll let you know more later, but could you do me a favour?"

"Of course, anything."

"Would you let his other friends know, the ones from college? What did he call you, the Ghoul Gang?"

"The Glue Club," said Paul slowly. "Of course I'll let them know."

"Thank you, Paul," she said, "you're so very kind. I'll speak to you again."

They said their goodbyes and Paul dropped the mobile on the floor, leaned forward and rubbed his face as hard as the pain in his forehead would allow him.

The screams got louder and Martin Edwards wondered how long it would be before Jenkins next door turned up his stereo to compensate. He hated listening to other people's music, especially Jenkins who seemed to like military marches and prog rock. Ellen, his wife, often told him to switch off and let it go but Martin couldn't and working from home didn't make it easier. Somebody would always start to mow their lawn when he needed to concentrate, or a lorry would back up, or somebody would sit in their car outside the house, the throbbing bass beats rattling the glass in the windows.

He stepped through the kitchen door onto the patio. "Girls! Who's murdering who?"

The screams stopped immediately. Carla, his eldest, stuck her pretty blonde head through the wendy house window. "What Daddy?"

"I said it sounds like you're killing each other in there, what's going on?"

Carla moved, frowned and then her little sister poked her head through. "Hey, Daddy."

"Hey Daisy."

"Did you want a cup of tea with us?" asked Carla.

"No thanks, I've got one here. I just wanted to make sure you're okay."

Daisy pulled her head back through the window. Carla watched her go, then looked at Martin. "Of course we are."

"Okay, see you in a bit."

"A bit," she said and disappeared from view. Within moments, they began talking and giggling loudly. Martin smiled, went back into the house and grabbed his mug of tea as he walked through to the study at the side of the house. His mobile was on the desk and, through force of habit, he checked it as he sat down. He had a missed call from 'Paul' and a new message, which he opened. 'Give me a call,' it read, 'we need to talk.'.

Martin sat down and rang his old friend.

"Thanks for getting back to me," Paul said, answering on the second ring as if he'd been waiting for the call.

"No problem, what's up?"

"Bad news I'm afraid and I wish I didn't have to tell you."

"Bad news?"

"Yes. Tom has died."

The words failed to compute. "Tom? But how?"

There was a pause, as if Paul was trying to work out what to say. "His Mum isn't sure, but it sounds like he drowned."

"Where?"

"Here in Gaffney."

Drowned in Gaffney? Tom was an adrenaline junkie who did risky things all over the world and he ends his days drowning in the town where he went to college? "How did that happen?"

"They don't know yet, but I thought you'd want to know. Will you come back for the funeral?"

Martin looked out of the window. A car went by soundlessly and tree branches moved in a gentle breeze. He could hear the girls in the garden but they seemed too far away, everything suddenly seemed too far away. "Yes, of course I will." Tom, the first bloke who'd spoken to him when he started at Gaffney Tech, the handsome stranger who'd introduced Martin to new people that would go on to become his closest friends over the next few years. How could he be gone? "Will you let me know?"

"I will."

"Thanks Paul." He was about to end the call, then

stopped. "And how are you, are you okay?"

Another pause. "I think so, thanks mate. Speak to you soon."

Paul put the phone down and took a deep breath. He'd thought he was doing okay but Martin asking if he was had made him realise he wasn't. There was a tightness across his chest, a lump he couldn't swallow and the headache was still jabbing his forehead.

He only had sisters but since the early days of Glue Club, Tom had taken to calling him brother and it had stuck, though only Paul continued to use the phrase as they moved through their twenties and thirties. Tom was an inspiring presence - and could occasionally be infuriating too - keeping in touch sporadically but Paul was always ready, willing to offer up a bed at the slightest opportunity. Jenny hadn't fallen under his spell completely - she'd liked him, of course because everyone who ever met him did, but she quickly tired of his sometimes juvenile humour, his 'don't worry be happy' attitude and his occasional big-brother-spitefulness towards Paul.

One call down, two to go. Should he tell any of them about the Pocock Factory, or leave it?

Jane Meadows looked up from the laptop screen as her mobile buzzed with an incoming message. She rolled her head from side to side, trying to work out the kinks in her neck that had set in as she compared data on a print-out with those on the system she was logged into. She looked across the office at her colleague Stan, who caught her eye and smiled, raising his eyebrows. To her side, the accounts manager whose system they were currently auditing didn't look at all comfortable and, based on some of the things she and Stan had found, shouldn't be.

She was glad they'd found something, even if it wasn't quite the deliberate misappropriation of funds the Head office had advised them it would be, though it didn't make up for them having spent four days in this hellhole of a regional branch on a bland industrial estate in Milton Keynes.

The text came from Paul Barrett, a blast from the past - they hadn't spoken in ages and she idly wondered where he'd got her number from.

Dear Jane, hope this finds you well. Could you give me a ring on 07852490571 as soon as you get a chance please? Thanks - speak to you soon, Paul.

"I have to make a call," she said to Stan and left the office, going downstairs to the car park where she'd get a bit of peace.

"Hello?"

"Paul? It's Jane, I got your message."

"Yes, thanks for phoning, I didn't have your number and I wasn't sure if you still used Facebook or not."

"Not often. What's up?"

"Well I wish this call could have been about happier circumstances but I have some bad news."

She looked up at the office window. The manager was watching her so Jane turned her back. "Go on."

"It's about Tom."

It had been a long time ago, she didn't want to react but couldn't help it. "What about him?"

"I'm sorry, Jane, but he's dead."

"Dead?" The word seemed to hang in front of her, as if refusing to enter the mouthpiece of the phone.

He let her silence run for a few moments. "His Mum

rang, they found him yesterday."

She tried to will herself into saying something but couldn't. Paul let the silence drift again and then coughed, as if embarrassed by the quiet. "Are you there?"

"Yes," she said, finally, "I just..."

"I know, it can't be easy with your history."

History. Not her first lover, but the first who'd actually meant something. The first to break her heart too. "It's not easy for anyone but that was a long time ago Paul."

"Will you come to the funeral?"

"Of course, let me know when you have the date."

"I will Jane. And for what it's worth, I'm sorry."

"Thank you."

Paul flicked through his contacts list on his phone until he found Gwen Chambers, the only one of the group - aside from Tom - he'd spoken to recently. He discovered she had a bakery business through Facebook and he'd got in touch when his parents celebrated their fiftieth wedding anniversary. They'd chatted easily on the phone, though when he tried to talk about the old days she'd clammed up, which confused him.

The phone rang as Gwen drove past the Fort Dunlop building and she ignored it, counting the rings until it went to voicemail. It was a chilly grey day, which was depressing enough, but following the stand-up argument she'd had with the shop manager in Marston Green, she wasn't in the mood for any more bad news. And all of a sudden, most of her life seemed to be filled with bad news.

Things still weren't right with her and Trevor, no

matter what he or Joe the couples counsellor said. The business, that little thing she'd been encouraged to launch five years ago, was now taking up so much of her time with management that if she got to spend a day a week baking she considered herself lucky. She didn't enjoy the meetings, she didn't enjoy the fact she spent so long driving backwards and forwards along this damned stretch of the M6 every week and she didn't enjoy having to repeatedly tell people that if a cake had her company name on it, then it had to be made to her recipe.

When did it all get so complicated?

She drove slowly into the tail end of the hold up for Spaghetti Junction and took a couple of deep breaths. She turned on the radio but Steve Wright was playing some modern tat that was all bass and repeated lyrics so she switched it off. The traffic came to a halt. She looked out of the window and saw the person in the next car picking their nose, index finger buried to the first knuckle. Charming.

She picked up her phone from the passenger seat and opened the voicemail, switching to loudspeaker.

"Hi Gwen, this is Paul Barrett from Gaffney. Could you give me a ring when you get this, I need to speak to you as soon as possible."

The message ended and she deleted it, staring at the screen. The wallpaper showed her and Trevor on Hunstanton beach with the sun behind them, a happy couple she didn't recognise. The traffic edged forward slightly but it was clear she was going to be stuck on the motorway for a while.

She rang Paul back and he answered within a few rings. "Hello, it's Gwen."

"Hello, thanks for getting back to me."

"No problem, how are you?"

"I could be better," he said. "I have bad news. Tom's passed away."

That would never have been her guess of what he was going to say. "Tom?"

"Yes, his Mum rang, they think he drowned."

The car in front pulled into the next lane which had started moving and Gwen eased up the clutch to fill the space. "Where?"

"In the canal here in Gaffney."

"What was he doing in Gaffney? I thought he was in Australia."

There was a pause, as if she'd caught him by surprise. "He was, but he went to Paris last week. How did you know?"

"He sent me a text from Sydney Harbour saying 'wish you were here.'"

"Sounds like him."

"Yes," she said, though now she'd never hear anything from him again. "When's the funeral?"

"They don't know yet, will you come back for it?"

"Yes, let me know."

"I will." He started to say something else but the traffic moved and she realised she didn't want to talk any more.

"I have to go, sorry."

"Take care, Gwen."

The connection was broken and as the car began to pick up speed, Gwen realised silent tears were falling onto her cheeks.

Chapter 3

The Gaffney Legendary Urban Explorers - the Glue Club for short - had been Tom's idea but, to Paul's way of thinking, most of the good ones back then were. A force of nature at Gaffney Tech, Paul had wanted to get to know him better from the moment he saw him across the crowded refectory, holding court about some pop band or another and bursting into bits of the song in question when it helped his argument. They had a couple of classes together - Tom confident, gregarious and hilarious, Paul much less so - fell into easy conversation and began to occupy a similar orbit. Away from the hubbub of social student life, Tom could be intense and serious, keen to ask questions and understand, fully aware Paul was smarter. Paul revelled in it, looking forward to the nights they sat up late, drinking and putting the world to rights. Both young men were interested in architecture, hated Brutalism and loved the Victorian factories that dotted Gaffney and when one was scheduled to be turned into flats, they decided to explore it. It had been a fun experience Tom was eager to repeat. He dropped a few hints, put up a couple of flyers and within a fortnight, he'd formed a club. Paul wasn't keen on the idea of sharing his new-found friend, but enjoyed the fact his social circle had widened and, after tolerating the two girls and other bloke, had grown to like them.

The club met infrequently, taking on perhaps three or four explorations in an academic year, but met for drinks two or three times a month.

Paul had missed the group ever since he left college and following Tom's death, he'd found it hard to focus on much else, as all thoughts of his old friend centred back towards the idea of urban exploration. It had been Paul who'd let Tom know about the Pocock Factory - for years, Tom's holy grail - and now it had somehow taken his life.

The idea played on his mind. He'd taken to going for a walk after his dinner and found, on most nights, his route took him past the Pocock factory to the canal. The first couple of times he'd tried to rationalise it - after all, wasn't it kind of ghoulish to visit the place his old friend had lost his life - but then just accepted it. There wasn't anything ghoulish about it, he just wanted to be here, to occupy the same space and pass on his best wishes.

When Tom's mum rang with the details of the funeral, the idea took further shape though it was another couple of nights before he had it clear enough in his mind what he wanted to say without telling everything.

That night, he sat at the small desk in the corner of the lounge and looked out the window at the common. A group of kids were playing football with far too many players on each side and the smallest child in goal. Older kids, perhaps late teenagers, were playing proper games on the pitches either side of them.

Turning his attention back to the flat, he looked at the line of photographs above the desk. Most were of family - in a fit of pique, he'd smashed his favourite of him and Jenny when the divorce papers came through - but he couldn't imagine ever taking down the one of his college friends.

Jane and Gwen were holding an A4 sheet of paper that Tom had scrawled Glue Club on and the three lads -

him, Tom and Martin - lined up behind them. They were all dressed for Urbex - dark clothes, helmets with torches and gloves - and all looked happy. The picture was taken, almost twenty years ago, on the night they explored Bentley's cinema on Russell Street. Locally notorious, a woman had been kidnapped and held there briefly before most of the building was destroyed in a fire. They'd found nothing unusual on their exploration, apart from a windowless room with glass all over the floor, but it had been exciting.

Glue Club and excitement, two things sadly lacking in Paul's life. He had a job he enjoyed, enough social life to keep him busy and a flat he didn't want but - thanks to the divorce settlement and having bought the family home at the right time - was mostly his. He missed the life and friends he'd had in college and was looking forward to seeing them again, though he'd have preferred any other circumstance to the one he found himself in - he still couldn't believe he'd never see Tom again.

He'd written a draft of the email that afternoon and now he was editing it, his fingers braced over the keyboard.

Hi all,

As everyone is coming to Gaffney for the funeral, I had a thought of how to give Tom a nice send-off. Do you remember back in the day, he was adamant that one day the Glue Club would explore the Pocock Factory near the canal? How about we do that for him? Nothing too strenuous, I'll provide the equipment, just a quick look around the building to say a final goodbye then we'll head for home.

What do you think?

All the best,
Paul

Was that any good? Would they share his enthusiasm? He looked out the window and saw the big game of football had broken up into several smaller games, which didn't even look like five-a-side.

The email wouldn't look any better if he left it five minutes or five hours, he decided and pressed send.

By ten o'clock they'd all responded, thanking him for a wonderful idea and a great gesture for an old friend.

Paul switched off his laptop and went for a bath.

Chapter 4

The girls stood at the front window with Ellen, waving as he walked down the garden path. The cabbie looked up from his paper and nodded. On the pavement, Martin turned. Ellen blew him a kiss and he returned it.

Carla, six and a veteran of the art of playing it cool, mouthed 'love you daddy' and waved. Daisy, two years younger and her eyes full of tears, waved as she tried to keep her bottom lip still. She'd had tears in her eyes since she got up, asking why Martin had to go away and when he'd be coming back. He'd explained, patiently, again and again that he had to go and say goodbye to his old friend. "But you have to say goodbye to me to say it to him," she'd said, with a cold logic he couldn't refute.

With a final wave, Martin got into the taxi and they set off. He hated being away from home.

The taxi got to St Pancras on time, the train was on schedule, his reserved seat wasn't already taken and nobody sat next to him as he sat by the window, headphones on and flicking through the latest copy of Photoshoot.

The train rolled into Gaffney a little over an hour later. The early mist had burned away and the mid-morning sky was a clear blue with a few wispy clouds.

Nobody else on his carriage got off and he stood on the platform as the train left, looking around and taking the old place in. The station had been smartened up since he was last here but still retained that old locked-in-the-seventies feel he'd noticed when he first arrived to start college.

Further up the platform, a woman stood with her back to him as she looked around. Another long-lost child of the town, he thought, as he grabbed his overnight case and headed for the stairway that would take him over the tracks to the ticket office. As he got closer, the woman extended the handle of her case and began to wheel it towards the stairwell. Martin adjusted his headphones and dropped back slightly, not wanting to crowd her but unless he stopped moving altogether he realised they would reach it together.

She turned at the last minute and he recognised her immediately. Recognition dawned in her eyes a moment or two later.

"Jane?" he said.

"Martin!" she said and they hugged, a little awkwardly. "How are you?"

"I'm okay, how about you?"

"Good, but I could murder a coffee."

"I'd love to buy you one," he said.

The coffee shop wasn't busy and the service was quick. Jane selected a table overlooking the platform and Martin put her Americano in front of her then sat in the chair opposite. They looked at one another and she smiled, a shy expression that seemed out of keeping.

"Have you been back much?" he asked.

"Hardly ever, I think the reunion a few years ago was the last time. How about you?"

"The same."

"Where are you living now?"

"Ealing," he said, "how about you?"

"Holland Park."

They were both on Facebook, he already knew this but it seems she didn't. He always expected people to keep up with social media as much as he did and was often surprised when they didn't. "How's your husband."

"Brian? He's very well, how about you, how's your…"

"Ellen," he said and smiled, saving her embarrassment. "She's very well thank you, working her way up the pecking order at Sotheby's."

Pursing her lips, Jane nodded. "Not bad. And how are the….?"

"Two children," he said and this time she shared his smile.

"I'm sorry," she said, "I just don't keep up with things. I set up a Facebook account because it was the thing to do but I can't remember the last time I went on it."

"Some people don't have them at all," Martin said. "My excuse is I work from home and it's easy to have it open on the laptop."

"What is it you do, something with photography?"

"I'm a commercial photographer. Sounds more glamorous than it is, I usually spend my days taking pictures of cans of food and trying to make them look desirable. What about you?"

"I'm a senior at an audit company," she said, "but it's not very glamorous. I spend a lot of time in bland offices, looking at lots of figures trying to find glitches." She sipped her coffee. "Anyway, you said you had two children."

"I do, Carla's six and Daisy's four."

"Do you enjoy fatherhood?"

"I love it. We decided, with our professions, that I'd be the stay-at-home so I spend a lot of time with them. Carla's at school so I don't see her during the day and Daisy's at nursery so I drop her off and then work. They know what I do, sometimes I let them help and it all works a treat."

"Very lucky."

"What about you, any kids?"

She pursed her lips and toyed with the lid of her coffee cup. "No, it was never the right time really and now, with both of us working and enjoying our income, it won't ever be."

"It could still happen."

She smiled but didn't look at him, concentrating on the lid. "Yeah, but that's not how things work is it?"

"No," he said, "not always."

They sat in silence for a few moments and Martin watched another train roll in and disgorge its passengers.

"I'm sorry," she said, "I'm not usually such a killjoy. It's good to see you again, Martin, it really is though I wish it was under better circumstances."

"Yes."

"I'm just, well, I don't know. Nervous isn't the right word but that's how I feel." She took another sip. "Tom's the first person my age to die, you know? He's my first friend to go, even if we hadn't been in touch for years. But we had a history and it feels wrong part of that's now gone." She worried the lid a bit more. "His parents were really young when they had him, I met them a few times and they didn't seem much older than us."

"I haven't seen them since we left college."

"I haven't seen Paul either, apart from at the reunion."

"I saw him a couple of times, mostly with Tom."

She nodded, watching the train leave. "So what do you think about the exploring?"

"Tonight? I'm hoping it'll be a laugh but it's been so long since I've done anything like that I'm not so sure."

"The Glue Club, eh?"

"Oh yes. Did you keep it up?"

"No. I looked at some groups when I was at University, then life got in the way and studying and all else and once Tom and I were finished, that kind of took away the last link I had with it. You?"

"Nah, I joined a group but it wasn't the same - the Glue Club, for me, was you lot, not what we did or where we explored. Without you four, I didn't enjoy it all that much so I got into running instead to keep fit."

"Well you look good." She was looking at him, as if properly for the first time since they'd seen one another. He smiled, looked at her. Always pretty, age had improved her. Her face was thin, with high cheekbones and big eyes. When she smiled, the luminosity radiated wide. There were lines around her eyes and mouth, which suited her unlike those on his own face and her dark brown hair was brushed away from her face.

"Thank you," he said, "you too."

She smiled, pressing her nail into the lid. "You know, I thought it would be awkward coming here but I'm so pleased I saw you on the platform, this has made me feel so much more comfortable."

"Good, same with me." And she was right, it was good to be going in with someone else.

She finished her coffee. "So how did it happen, did you hear any more from Paul?"

"No, nothing new."

"Was he in any trouble?"

He smiled. "Same thing I thought. I suppose we'll find out soon."

Jane looked at her watch. "Yes, I need to find my hotel and get changed."

"Where are you staying?"

"The Premier Inn, in town. How about you?"

"The same. We'll share a taxi there and take one to the crematorium if you want."

Jane nodded. "Yes," she said, "I'd like that very much."

The hotel room was clean and functional, which pleased her. With practised ease, she unpacked the items that needed to be hung - her funeral suit and blouse - and put her washbag in the bathroom. Kicking off her shoes, she put the kettle on and sat on the bed, laid back quickly and put her arms out to her sides - yes, it was comfortable and not too soft - then sat up and rubbed her feet as she waited for the water to boil. When it had, she made a cup of strong coffee, carried it to the window and looked out over Gaffney High Street.

People moved with purpose - mothers pushing buggies or walking slowly with toddlers, connected by hands and smiles; men and women in suits, looking as if they were rushing to the next important meeting but were probably racing to get to Costa for their caffeine fix; students wasting their free periods; older couples, hand-in-hand or arm-in-arm, taking the day easy and window shopping. It was a High Street like any other but one she hadn't seen in a long time and she felt the pull of the past.

Her phone beeped with a message from Martin: *The taxi is booked, I'll meet you in reception in ten minutes if that's okay?*

She replied 'yes,' drank some coffee and went into the bathroom to freshen up and get dressed. Life on the road had taught her expedience and she was in reception before he got there. She watched him come down the stairs and smile as he saw her.

"You were quick."

"I'm a practised hand," she said, standing up. He was wearing a black suit, a white shirt with a dark blue tie and he carried it well. His hair was thinning but still mostly brown, his face was lean and his jawline, where he'd recently shaved, looked smooth and young. His eyes, blue and playful, hadn't changed in the past twenty years - she'd never had a romantic notion about Martin but had always got on well with him and it pleased her to see him looking so fit and healthy now.

"Obviously," he said and held out his left arm. She linked her right through it and they went out of reception together.

The sky above Gaffney Crematorium was cloudless and birds sang in the trees lining the car-park. The taxi pulled onto a small roundabout and they got out, Martin paying the fare against her objections. They stood together and watched it drive away.

There were two chapels in front of them, the smaller one facing the roundabout, the larger, more gothic-looking one next to the car park. Several narrow paths cut across the well maintained lawns to a burial area which opened out behind the chapels.

"Are you ready?" Martin asked.

"As I'll ever be," Jane said.

A small group of people were standing in the porch of the smaller chapel but she didn't recognise any of them.

They crossed the roundabout and Jane noticed a woman standing on her own with her back to the car park. Short and slim, she wore dark sunglasses, a black dress that hung below her knee and black tights.

"Is that Gwen?" she asked Martin.

He looked over. "Yeah, I think so."

"We should say hello."

Gwen saw them as they reached the pavement, a quick smile flashing across her face and brightening it considerably. She hugged Jane fiercely, Martin less so and then stood back.

"You look so good," she said, looking them both up and down.

"You too," said Martin.

Jane held Gwen's shoulders. "It's good to see you."

"It's been a while, hasn't it?"

"For all of us," said Martin. "Have you seen Paul?"

"No, but I only got here a few minutes ago, I haven't seen anyone."

"Did you know Tom's parents?" Jane asked.

"I might recognise them, but I'm not sure."

"Well, we'll go and see if they're over there," Jane said, nodding towards the mourners.

Martin looked over towards the car park and saw Paul walking across the grass. "You go," he said, "I'll catch you up."

He watched Jane and Gwen walk away then went to intercept Paul, who extended his hand and gave a hearty shake.

"It's good to see you, Martin."

"Likewise. The girls have gone to find Tom's parents."

"They both came?"

"Yes, the gang's all gathered."

"Shame it had to be like this," said Paul slowly. Martin looked at him and realised his eyes were glistening.

"Come on, mate."

"Ah, I know," said Paul, twisting his face into a grimace briefly. "It's just, fuck it, you know? He didn't deserve to die, he wasn't bloody old enough."

"You're right."

"And if I hadn't told him about Pocock's..."

"What about it?"

Paul looked towards the mourners. "I'll tell you later, it looks like we're being assembled."

Martin glanced over and saw two tall men in dark suits with their arms spread, as if trying to corral a group of sheep through a pen. "Yes, come on."

When the service ended, Martin left the chapel with Jane and Gwen, who he'd sat with. Paul had sat on the second row behind Tom's parents and met them on the patio as family members and friends walked around hugging one another and offering condolences. Martin hugged Tom's mum and shook his dad's hand. The man nodded, mumbled thanks then looked away with watery eyes.

The four of them edged away from the main throng of bodies - they'd known Tom and been close friends but that didn't cut it here, with the family and history links.

"I was thinking," said Paul, "how about, before we go to Pocock's, we nip to the Raj for a curry?"

"That surely can't still be in business?" asked Jane.

"It was a Health & Safety Inspector visit away from being closed when we used to go in there," said Martin and Jane laughed, then looked around guiltily.

"Oh it's a lot grander now," said Paul.

Chapter 5

It wasn't a lot grander than Martin remembered. Back then, there were booths with veneer chipped off the tables, terrible flock wallpaper, a huge fishtank built into one wall with the occasional floating corpse and a lot of photographs of patrons and staff. The booths were still there, though the tables looked neater, the wallpaper had no geometric shapes but peeled near the ceiling and there were still lots of photographs. The fishtank now had lights in it which made it look grander and he couldn't see any bodies floating on the surface. The music was as loud as he remembered, though it was now 80s hits played on a sitar.

"Ah, Mr Barratt," said the man behind the counter when they went in.

"Alright Sami? I have a table for four."

"Of course, follow me."

They threaded their way through to the far corner of the restaurant, where they were seated in front of a large window giving them a good view of the high street.

"See," said Paul, "it's a lot grander."

After a few moments of trying to decide whether to order a set meal, their own choices or to share, the waiter asked for their drinks and left, giving them another five minutes to make a decision on the food. When the drinks arrived, Paul watched them handed out with rapt attention and smiled at the waitress as she left.

"So," he said and held his pint glass in the air, "I

Mark West

would like to bring this sad meeting of Glue Club to order."

Martin raised his own glass, waiting for Jane and Gwen to raise theirs. "Not the reunion we wanted, but it's good to see you all again."

"Yes," said Paul quickly, as if annoyed with Martin's comment, "thanks for coming."

"Of course," said Jane, "I wouldn't miss this."

Gwen put her glass down and rubbed under her chin with the top of her left hand. "Glue Club," she said, "now there's a name I've not heard in a long time. Do you remember when Tom was going to get us all t-shirts made?"

"Until he realised how much it would cost," said Martin.

"Is that why we never got them?" asked Jane and the others laughed.

"We got badges instead, do you remember?" said Gwen.

"Those tiny things nobody could read," nodded Martin.

"I stopped wearing mine after about an hour, it looked like everyone was staring at my tits," said Jane.

"We should have worn them tonight," said Paul.

"I have no idea where mine is," said Martin.

"Or me," said Gwen.

"I threw mine away after Mr Hudson used it as an excuse to leer at my left boob," said Jane.

"Oh," said Paul and Martin looked at him, suddenly aware that Paul not only had his badge but knew exactly where it was.

The waitress came back and patiently took their food orders, even though all of them - except Paul - changed their minds at least once. When she left, the table fell silent for a few moments as if everyone was aware they wanted to talk about their missing friend but didn't quite know how to broach the subject.

"The service was nice," said Jane, after a while and the others nodded in agreement with her.

"You know, it sounds silly to say 'I didn't think this would happen' but I genuinely didn't with Tom," said Paul.

"He did have that way about him," nodded Jane, taking a big gulp of her wine.

"I take it he never stopped living and partying hard?" said Martin.

"Not that I ever saw," said Paul. "I think not getting married was part of it, he had no ties. When I was with Jenny, he'd ring up at odd times and suggest an adventure that involved me being away from home, at a moments notice, for days at a time."

The waitress came back with a stack of poppadoms and a condiment holder and put them in the centre of the table.

Jane took a popadom and broke it in half on her plate, then spooned some onion onto it. "I thought he'd calm down, you know, but it didn't happen."

"But he had a responsible job, didn't he?" asked Gwen.

"He was a consultant," said Paul, "which gave him a great excuse to travel."

Martin reached for a popadom. "And allowed him to pursue his sports in new environments?"

Paul smiled. "He got a contract that took him to Cortina for a while and got into snowboarding."

Martin laughed. "I worry about slipping over when

it's icy and breaking something, he was the same age and got into snowboarding?"

"Yes. He was a qualified scuba diver, did a bit of mountain climbing and hill running in Wales, I don't think I ever met anyone with as much energy."

"Energy," said Martin, "absolutely. "The last time I saw him was a few months ago, he was in London for a conference and we went for a drink."

"He never said," said Paul and Martin looked at him. There was something there, beyond the idea of him holding onto the past with the badge - had he perhaps read more into the friendship than was really there? Did he believe Tom was his best friend? As Paul noticed the others watching him, colour hit his cheeks and he looked at his plate, reaching for a popadom and breaking it in half.

"He was in town for a few days," Martin said, "and wanted to have a bit of fun. We arranged to meet in the City, had a drink and a meal then he was on about going to a club and getting some Paintball in on the Sunday. Full of energy."

"All natural?" asked Jane.

"Tom didn't take drugs," said Paul too quickly and more colour tinged his cheeks.

"Okay," she said then, to Martin, "so did you go?"

"Paintball? No. Ellen was in the middle of a big thing at work and needed to go in on the Sunday and as much as my girls would love to go out to a forest for the afternoon, I wasn't taking them. Plus I got the idea Tom wasn't so keen on kids, he asked me vaguely about my family but not much."

"I think he tended to cut off from things that didn't specifically interest him," said Jane.

"Don't we all do that?" asked Paul.

"Yes, but..."

"We've just been to his funeral, you know, maybe now isn't the time to start dismantling him."

"I'm not dismantling him, Paul, I'm just saying."

"That he didn't care."

"No, not that he didn't care, but he only listened to things he wanted to."

Paul shook his head but said nothing.

"I think Jane's right," said Martin, "that's why Tom he lived like he did, he had a focussed set of priorities."

"That's not dismantling him," said Gwen slowly.

"No," said Jane "and I say this from experience. When we were together, if something didn't affect him, or us as a couple, it didn't register."

"I still think that's harsh," said Paul.

Jane turned to face him directly. "How is that harsh?" she demanded.

"Hey," said Gwen, "let's not fall out."

"I'm not going to fall out, I just don't understand why it's harsh. I lived with the bloke for two years, I knew him pretty well and that's my opinion. Martin said he didn't pay much attention to talk of his family, it's just the way he was."

Paul looked at her. "I'm sorry, okay, I shouldn't have said it, I'm just feeling..."

"We're all feeling it, mate," said Martin.

The waitress came over, saw the popadoms were gone and made a gesture that brought two waiters, one to clear the table, the other to place hot-plates in the centre. The conversation stopped as they waited for the food, motioning towards themselves as the waitress picked up each dish. When she was done, they thanked her and she left.

"Looks lovely," said Gwen.

"I'm starving," said Jane.

Apart from complimenting their food - and occasionally offering bites to each other - nobody spoke as they ate. Martin, glad the potential bad atmosphere between Paul and Jane had been defused, watched them both as they ate. Jane seemed fine, quick to smile but Paul was clearly carrying something else within him and he wished he could figure it out. If there was something he could say or do, to make his friend feel more comfortable about the situation, then he'd do it.

When they finished, Paul called the waitress over and they ordered more drinks as the waiters took away their plates and balti bowls.

"Very nice," said Martin, "a fitting way to say goodbye to an old friend."

"He did like his curry," agreed Paul.

"Do you remember the phal that time?" asked Martin. "Some tosser came in, saying he could eat a hotter curry than anyone else in here."

Jane laughed. "We told him not to do it."

"I don't think Tom could ever refuse a challenge," said Paul.

"You know, he told me he couldn't taste anything for the best part of three days," said Gwen.

"But he won," said Paul, "and that was all that he wanted."

"So what was he doing here?" asked Jane, "why did he come back?"

Paul looked around the table. "It was all my fault, actually, I emailed him about the Pocock Factory and he was all over it."

"I thought it was locked," said Martin.

"The old lady died," said Paul. "Almost as soon as she did, the place went up on the market and the plot's been bought for luxury waterside apartments."

"That was quick," Jane said.

"Within a couple of weeks," Paul said.

"So why hadn't he been in there before?" asked Martin. "Surely kids must have broken into it?"

Paul shook his head. "Nobody apparently. It was locked up tight, apparently alarmed and every now and again, you'd see a bloke doing a perimeter check with a bloody great big Alsatian on a lead at his side."

"And now none of that's there?"

"No. The fencing stayed up but the guarding sign was taken down. I left it five days, found a piece of fence that had been," he cleared his throat, "adjusted and I was in."

"I could never understand why he was always so keen to go in there," said Martin.

"I don't know if it was the building or the history," said Gwen.

"What do you mean?" asked Jane.

"Well you know, the ghost stories about the place." Paul made a noise somewhere between a laugh and snort of derision but she ignored him. "Don't you remember him going on about it, he loved the idea there was this haunted building in town he could explore and debunk."

"What were the ghost stories?" asked Jane.

"From when it started up, years back. My granddad worked there before the war and he said there were a lot of stories, especially about how awful old man Pocock had been. Apparently you could sometimes hear kids crying in corridors, or people shouting, it was proper scary."

45

"I never knew any of this," said Martin, "did your granddad see or hear anything?"

"He heard the kids crying and one of his friends was in an office and heard someone coming up the stairs but nobody was there."

"Wow," said Jane.

"I'm not sure whether any of that's true," said Paul, "but Tom really wanted to get in. I emailed him, said that it was now accessible and he arranged to come down but I got walloped by a twenty-four-hour bug and then he died."

"But you said he drowned," Martin pointed out.

"That's what's they said."

"So how did he get from the factory into the canal?"

"Maybe he never got into the factory," said Jane, "maybe he was walking around the outside to have a look and fell in."

"Well there's apparently no suspicious circumstances," said Paul.

The waitress came back with their drinks and handed them out.

"Can't be nice for his parents, not really knowing," said Gwen.

"It's often the way," said Martin.

"Did he keep up with the Urbex?" asked Jane. "You said he was into adrenaline stuff, did he keep his hand in with the buildings?"

"I think so," said Paul.

"He didn't say much when I saw him," said Martin.

"I know he did some this year," said Gwen and coloured up when they all looked at her. "He was in Wolverhampton in early February and asked if I'd join him."

"Why did he ask you?" asked Paul and Martin glanced at him.

"Because I'm in Birmingham I suppose," she said.

"And did you go?" Paul asked.

Gwen tilted her head to one side and lifted her wineglass to her mouth but didn't drink. There was an unreadable expression on her face and Martin thought she wasn't going to answer. She bit her lip then set her head straight. "No, I haven't done that in years."

"None of us have," said Jane.

"I have," said Paul quickly.

"Well I haven't," said Gwen, "so I said no and then he wanted to meet up."

"You say that like you didn't go," said Martin.

She looked at him, a neutral gaze that nevertheless quickly became uncomfortable. "I thought about it but, you know, there were things."

"Things?" asked Paul. Martin glanced at him, amazed at how the man could misread situations so badly.

"Yes Paul," said Gwen, "things. A bit of history."

Jane steepled her fingers and rested her chin on them. "When?"

"Long after you," Gwen smiled.

Jane reached across the table and touched the back of her friend's hand. "I didn't doubt it for a second."

"It was about five years ago, he called me out of the blue..."

"Did he ever do anything but?" asked Martin and the others nodded.

"I don't think so," Gwen said with a faint smile. "It was a bad time, at work and at home and he got me at the worst possible moment - for me, that is. We went for a drink, got a bit too loaded. The conversation was easy and the memories were pleasant and he was staying in town and, well, one thing led to another." She looked at her index finger and worried the nail with her tooth for a moment. "There was a building in town that was just about to be torn down and he wanted to check it out but needed a second. I told him I hadn't done it in years and so we spent the weekend in his hotel room instead." She looked at her glass, then at each of her friends in turn. "And that was that."

"You didn't see him again?" asked Jane.

"No, just the odd catch-up on Facebook."

"That's how life gets sometimes," said Martin.

"Maybe," said Gwen.

"So nobody but Paul has done any Urbex since Glue Club then?" asked Martin.

"When did you last go?" Jane asked.

"Last year. Tom found out about an old factory unit that was being knocked down and we had a look around. It was enjoyable and something I hope to get into more, now that there's just me, you know? Everyone needs a hobby and all that." He smiled. "But you all seem good and fit, so there shouldn't be any problems tonight."

"Well we're not doing anything dangerous, are we?" asked Gwen.

"You said we'd just have a wander," Jane pointed out.

"Oh we will, nothing dangerous at all. I've got all the kit we need in the car, we'll go in and walk around for Tom and then head for home."

"Take nothing but photographs, leave nothing but footprints," said Martin.

"Precisely. I mean, the worst thing that could happen is one of us trips and twists an ankle. We've all got mobiles, I've got some digital walkie-talkies and torches, we'll be fine."

Jane looked out of the window. "Dusk is coming," she said, "I take it we're not going in until it's dark?"

Paul looked out too. "I think that's for the best. Did you want to leave your car here and I'll take you all back to your hotels so you can get changed?"

"Makes sense," Gwen nodded.

"Then let's go and explore," said Paul.

Chapter 6

It was a cloudless evening. A three-quarter moon hung in the navy sky surrounded by stars and only the faintest burnt orange embers of the day lingered on the horizon.

Shelley Street was quiet. Martin, Jane, and Gwen stood across from the factory, in front of an old peoples home that was showing signs of wear and neglect. To their right, creating a dead end, were three large buildings that all had broken windows and tattered 'For Sale' signs stuck to them, waiting patiently for the urban regeneration that would surely come. There were a handful of cars outside the residential houses at the other end of the street but only three here, one of which was canted at an angle since it lacked the nearside front wheel.

"It doesn't look like I remember it," said Jane.

"It looks sad," said Gwen.

"Do you think that's because it knows it's going to be turned into a block of flats?" asked Jane with a smile. Gwen returned the smile but didn't say anything.

Martin stepped back further, to take the whole building in. Built of red brick that looked rusty in the shadowy light, it stood five feet back from the pavement and was three storeys high. Eight arched leaded windows lined the top floor, seven on the first floor along with a loading door and five half-size windows on the ground floor. A door that looked far too small to be useful was in the far left corner and two small windows were next to it. Metal mesh fencing, in panels eight or nine feet tall, were concreted into the ground and barred the factory from the road.

"Still looks locked up tight to me," he said.

Jane pointed to the right of the building. "Down there leads to the canal, so I imagine that's where the side entrances are."

Gwen looked towards the mouth of Shelley Street, where Paul had parked and was now getting equipment from the boot. "What is he doing? If we loiter here long enough, it's going to be suspicious."

"Hardly," said Martin, gesturing toward the dead end, "who's here to see us?"

"It makes you wonder why they had security guards and alarms," said Jane.

"Maybe there were jewels hidden in the walls and under the floorboards," said Gwen.

"Calm down, Nancy Drew," said Martin, "here he comes."

Paul stopped in front of them and adjusted the large holdall that was slung over his shoulder.

"What kept you?" asked Gwen.

"Sorry," he said and patted the bag, "just getting the kit. It pays to be prepared." He looked at them all and nodded that they'd dressed to his instructions - dark fleeces, jeans and walking boots. "Come on, it only takes one old dear to look out her window and make a comment that people are afoot in the night."

He led them to the fence just beyond the corner of Pocock's. Several links had been broken near to the bottom of the last panel but pushed back so they looked untouched. He pushed them out with his foot so the others could crawl through then Martin held the mesh up for him. Beyond was a narrow passage, twice as wide as a pavement, which ran between Pocock's and the factory next to it, the brick canyon deep in shadow.

"Mind your step," Paul advised and switched on a penlight torch, its narrow beam illuminating the cracked concrete.

The path dropped at a slight angle and ahead, the canal was little more than an oily smear of moonlight. The other building was a blank wall, with a few windows just below the roofline and Martin looked up at Pocock's. There were more arched windows here and a wooden door on each floor at the end of the building, with a hoist arm attached above them. A set of double-doors, at ground level, were halfway along the path and Paul stopped in front of them.

"We're going in here," he said, gesturing at the doors. A sign above them read 'Workers Entrance'. The door looked solid, with no windows and there was a big padlock in a hasp.

"Well that could be interesting, unless you have a key," said Jane.

"I do," said Paul and brandished one in his hand with all the flair of an end-of-pier magician.

"How the fuck did you manage that?" asked Martin.

Paul turned and the torchlight on his face caught a sly smile. "Because I snipped off the original one and replaced it."

"Very sneaky," said Gwen, "I like it."

"Thanks." He slipped the holdall off his shoulder and unzipped it on the ground. Reaching in, he said "Safety first" and handed them each a dark bump cap.

Martin took his. A headtorch was attached just above the peak. He switched it on and the others did the same, looking at each other and blinding themselves, which caused a quick outbreak of giggling. Some of it, Martin felt, was because of the stupidity of the situation but some of it was the atmosphere. In the Raj and out on Shelley Street, this was an almost abstract concept, that they would take up urban exploring the best part of twenty years since they'd last done it. But standing here in the heavy shadow, dwarfed by the buildings they stood between, there was a chill that wasn't only physical. For the first time, since he'd told Ellen of Paul's plan and she'd laughed, convinced he was joking, Martin wasn't sure if this was a good idea.

"Do you feel that?" he asked no-one in particular, keen to both voice the question and break the tension.

"Of being hemmed in?" asked Gwen.

"Yes," said Jane.

"Of course we're hemmed in," said Paul, "we're in an alleyway."

"No," said Jane, "it's more than that."

"Is it safe?" Martin asked.

Paul barked out a quick laugh. "Safe?"

"Yes," said Jane. "We're not kids anymore."

"It's safe and the equipment will make it more so. The building's been shut up tight as a drum since the mid-80s and all we do is go in, head upstairs, take some pictures and get out."

"Do you have a floor plan?" asked Martin.

"No, we just stick to the staircases against whichever wall they start on, so we can always get our bearings." He reached into the holdall and took out several packs of gloves. "I didn't know your sizes," he said apologetically. "There are regular leather ones to put on now and some latex ones too, just in case."

Jane looked at Martin, raised her eyebrows and

mouthed 'latex?' Martin smiled.

"I doubt there'll be much mobile reception in there so I've got some digital walkie-talkies," he said and handed them out. Martin took his, which fitted into the palm of his hand. "They haven't got much range, but they work," Paul continued. "Then these are your own backpacks, with supplies." He handed them all four narrow packs. "Back-up torches, elbow and kneepads, a mini First Aid kit and chalk, just in case we get split up. They're all different colours."

Gwen took out her kneepads. "I wear short skirts at work," she said, "I don't want my knees all knackered."

"Quite," Paul said. "There's also a dust mask, a GPS locator attached to the backpack flap, some wet wipes and a multi-tool, just in case."

"Very prepared," said Martin.

Paul nodded, as if unsure of how to take the compliment. He waited as everyone put their pads on and slid the backpacks over their shoulders. "Are we ready?" he asked.

He helped them hook up the headsets and Martin put his multi-tool in his fleece pocket.

"As we'll ever be," said Jane.

"What's the worst that could happen?" asked Gwen.

"Precisely," Paul said. He opened the padlock, released the hasp and pushed the door. It swung open with only mild protest, grit catching underneath it. "Here we go," he said and stepped into the darkness.

Chapter 7

The hallway they stepped into was clearly just a holding area for the workers. There were no windows but three clockcard machines were on either wall and, ahead, was a set of double-doors with glass panels over them. The ceiling was panelled and darkened by nicotine and four light fixtures, their bulbs dirty and blackened, hung down. The floor was carpeted with white dust and grit.

"I'm going to shut the door," said Paul.

Martin heard one of the girls say "okay" as the moonlight was slowly crowded out and then it was just their head torches. The way the beams jerked and jumped, as people moved, made him feel suddenly nauseous and he looked at the floor.

Paul put a hand on his back. "You okay mate?"

"Yeah, just a bit disorientated."

"It's the lights," said Jane.

"I'm feeling a bit queasy too," said Gwen.

"It's just been so long since I've done this," said Martin.

"You're not used to it," said Paul, "that's all. This room is small, the others won't be and you'll feel better."

He led the way to the double doors, Jane and Gwen behind him, Martin bringing up the rear. Embarrassed he'd made a fuss, he kept his gaze along the side wall just in case the worst happened and he did throw up.

Paul pulled the door but it didn't move. He pushed it to no avail.

"Is it locked?" asked Gwen.

"Hardly," he said and tried it again.

"So how were you and Tom going to get in?"

"This way."

She pushed the door herself. "So there's no other way in?"

"Well there might be, it's an old building so it's not going to be that secure, but I did a couple of circuits and apart from a few smashed windows, I couldn't see any kind of opening, door or window."

"I'm amazed," said Gwen, "that an empty factory could escape vandalism, especially being out of the way like this."

"So was I," Paul admitted, "but you can see it for yourself. Those guards must have been pretty good."

"Or had big dogs," said Jane.

"Try it again," said Gwen.

Paul pushed and pulled on the door hard enough they all heard something click near the hinges.

"One more go," said Gwen.

Martin stood next to him and, together, they pushed the door until the same thing clicked and it swung open onto a dark space.

"Corridor," said Paul.

"But you don't have a floorplan?" asked Jane.

"No, I looked everywhere I could possibly think of one."

"Maybe you should have looked harder," she said and exchanged a look with Gwen. Martin looked at Paul, who was staring into the darkness, oblivious. Something about this didn't feel right and it was clear they shared his feeling. It wasn't really the lack of a floorplan, but he couldn't put his finger on the nagging feeling.

"So where now?" he asked.

"This will be an access corridor that leads to the factory and the reception area. We head through and up to the first floor, have a look around the offices and then go up again if we can. Get some pictures, enjoy the view and then we come back."

"What if the layout isn't like that?" asked Jane.

Paul turned, exasperated, his torch beam shining in her face. "I don't know, Jane, alright? I tried to find the information but couldn't though going by other factories in the area, the layout will be similar."

"Hey, Paul, take it easy," said Martin.

Paul looked at him, blinding him with his torch. Martin held his hand up to shield the light.

"I asked you because you organised it," said Jane, her voice steely.

"You could have looked it up," Paul said.

"If you'd asked me to, I would have."

"Hey, it shouldn't be up to me..."

"Enough," said Gwen. "For fucks sake, Paul, you asked us to do this, you've organised the kit and it's only reasonable to expect you to have a floorplan."

He looked at her and then at the floor. "Okay, I'm sorry, alright? I fucked up. I just thought it'd be a treat to Tom."

"And it is," said Martin, "but it'd be nice to see where we're going. We're none of us spring chickens anymore."

There was silence for a moment, then Gwen said, "you speak for yourself," which made Jane and Martin laugh.

"The layout will be the same, I'm convinced of it. I tell you what, if we don't come to the reception area at the end of this corridor, we'll turn around. Okay Jane?"

She looked at him, her beam playing on his cheek.

"Yes."

"And I'm sorry," he said, without looking at her.

"Apology accepted."

He nodded and went through the doorway, Jane and Gwen following him, Martin bringing up the rear.

The corridor was very dark and Gwen looked at her feet to avoid the nausea she knew the bobbing torch lights would give her. Briefly she wondered how Martin was doing behind her and hoped he wasn't sick on her back.

The floor was gritty and she could see marks from Paul and Jane's shoes. There were other footprints too, dusted over now and she wondered how long it had been since they were made.

The lights ahead stopped.

"Found a door," called Paul and she heard it open, his torch beam playing against the wall.

"What is it?" called Martin.

"Changing rooms."

"Let's move on," said Jane and they did.

When she got to the door, Gwen opened it and peered in. Wooden benches lined the walls, with hooks set into the wall a few feet above them. She wondered which one her granddad had used, what the banter in this room was like before and after a shift. If she held her breath, she wondered if she could perhaps hear them? She'd loved the old man and would do anything to listen to his deep voice and booming laugh again.

"Anything exciting?" asked Martin. She stepped into the room so he could see.

"Just curious," she said, "you know, my granddad."

She stepped back into the corridor and closed the door behind her.

"What did he do?"

"He was a clicker."

"A what?"

"He cut the uppers for the shoes."

"A lost art, I presume."

"I imagine so."

He nodded. "Another thing we've lost. We lose skills, old friends and we'll soon lose this building."

"That's progress."

He made a light sound, to show he found her comment amusing. "That's one way of putting it."

They fell into step in silence, not in any hurry to catch up with the others. She wanted to ask why he was here, in this old building, in a town he'd long since left behind. Was it really just to honour an old friend? Could there be any other reason? If it hadn't been for her granddad and some of the old stories he'd told her, she doubted she'd have come on this foolish adventure, Tom or no Tom.

"Another door," called Paul. He waited until Gwen and Martin caught up and then pushed it open slowly. The area beyond was so large their torches didn't reach the far wall and the moonlight that came through the windows only showed them a hazy impression of the dimensions of the space.

"Can you see much?" asked Martin.

"Looks like the rough cutting room," said Paul, moving his head to pan his beam. "There are a load of presses and some work benches."

"And wicker baskets," said Jane.

"They used them to carry material around the factory."

Martin leaned through the doorway and peered around, then Gwen took her turn. "So where did the

Clickers work?"

"That'd be upstairs, we'll go and have a look."

Paul shut the door and they continued along the corridor. Soon, Gwen could see the faintest glow of a door outline ahead of them. Nobody said anything. The silence, in the darkness, was quite a pleasant situation though she knew it was only bearable because she wasn't alone. Her mind wandered and she thought of her granddad. A gregarious, happy man who loved to be the life and soul of the party, he became a little melancholic when he was in his cups, as her grandma liked to call those drunken aftermaths. After one such occasion, when she was in her early teens and an avid fan of supernatural stories, she asked him if he'd ever seen a ghost.

"Maybe," he'd said, "once or twice."

She'd looked deeply at him, trying to see in his eyes if he was joking her. "Really?"

"Uh huh, that was one of the joys of working at Pocock's."

"What happened there?"

"What didn't, little lady? It was a good place, I suppose, because it gave me a profession and it paid for me and your grandma so that we could have your Dad and then he could have you."

"But it was haunted?"

"You could say that. Lots of noises, some things we saw, people we heard."

Paul and Jane stopped in front of her, stirring Gwen from her memory.

"This should lead to reception," said Paul and tried the handle. Jane turned her head slightly, catching Gwen in her beam. Martin brought his hand up to shield his eyes.

"Sorry," she said.

"Don't worry about it."

Jane turned back as Paul pushed the door open. It went easily, the bottom catching grit as it passed over the black and white floor tiles. She followed him into the reception area, which was a large square space with windows above the main doors to their left letting in soft moonlight. Across from them was a double glass panel, a sign above it reading 'Reception'. Under it was a small leather sofa, coated in dust and the long-dead remains of a plant, mummified in a dry and crusted pot. There were large pictures on the walls and the closest to her showed horses grazing in a field. Paul went to look at another but she couldn't make out the image. On the wall to the right were two doors, one marked 'Offices'.

"Not too many people been through here recently," said Martin, training his beam on the floor. The dust and grit was thick and theirs were the only footprints Jane could see.

"So where did the guards come in then?" she asked.

Paul stepped back from the painting. "I don't know that they ever had a need to come in."

"Unless there's another entrance," suggested Gwen.

"Perhaps a broken window around the back, near the canal maybe?" said Jane. "I mean, a site this big, you'd think somebody would get in."

"But if they did," Martin said, "surely there'd be graffiti and litter. Think back to some of the places we used to go."

"Regular art galleries," said Paul, nodding. The movement made his torch beam glint off the picture, throwing strange shapes against the leather sofa.

"I haven't seen anything like that yet. And the dust on

the floor is," Martin paused, as if searching for the right word, "pristine."

"Which makes this all that much more special," said Paul, "a more fitting memory to Tom. Let's head upstairs."

"When was it closed up?" asked Jane.

"Back in the eighties, I think," Gwen said, "I remember granddad talking about it when he retired."

"Yeah," said Martin, "I meant to ask you about that. Back in the Raj, you were saying he told stories about the place."

"Uh huh, from back before the war. Little ghost stories, you know, things happening that nobody could explain."

"I read some of them," said Paul, "when I was looking into the place. Superstition and stories to scare the newbies, like asking them to go and get some tartan paint."

"I don't know," said Gwen, "Granddad was quite certain."

"Well let's hope there aren't any ghosts around now," said Jane. "I'm a fortysomething woman who audits for a living and I'm still not sure I'm up to this Urbex. I certainly don't want to encounter anything that goes bump in the night."

Martin laughed.

Chapter 8

The door opened onto a narrow staircase and Paul led the way up, Gwen behind him. Jane looked at Martin and raised her eyebrows.

"Do you have a bad feeling about this?"

"I don't have a good one," he said.

She smiled and he followed her up the stairs which opened into another reception area. Across the space were glass-panelled double doors and the wall to their right was filled with windows looking out onto darkness. Three doors were on the left and, just to the side of them, two leather sofas hugged the wall. Paul had walked to the furthest door on the left and he called back "Managing Director" when he reached it.

"Factory Manager," said Gwen, standing at the next door.

There was enough light that Martin didn't have to get closer to the remaining door to read the legend on it. "MD Secretary," he said.

"So this was the bigwigs area," said Paul and looked at the double-doors. Martin could see there was a sign on it too but couldn't make it out.

"Offices," Paul said, "must be through here."

Jane went to the windows and cupped her hands around her eyes, leaning against the glass. "Can't see much," she said, "apart from benches."

"That'll be the Clicking room," Paul said, heading for the office door, "where Gwen's granddad worked."

"I want to go and see that," she reminded him.

"We will," he said and pushed the doors, propping them open against the walls.

The corridor stretched further than their torch beams and there were no glass panels above any of the doors to let in light from outside. Thick strands of cobweb hung from the light fitting in front of them and the floor was white with dust.

"Nobody been through here in a while either," said Jane.

They all looked at Paul who winced in the light. "I imagine," he said, "the offices will run along the length of the building and there must be a staircase at the other end to get to the third floor."

"Could you go up a floor through the Clicking room?" Martin asked.

"That'd make sense," Paul said, nodding.

"I'm going to have a look in the office," said Jane.

"I'll come with you," Paul said and they moved off towards the nearest office door. Gwen moved too, heading towards the double-doors for the Clicking room on the right.

The first office door opened with a creak, making him jump. Paul and Jane both turned towards him and he shielded his eyes.

"Sorry," said Jane. "Didn't know it'd make a noise."

He waved his hand at her. "Anything in there?"

"Bits and pieces. Come and look."

He realised he didn't really want to, nor did he want to look at the Clicking room. His passion for urban exploration had dulled over the years and this expedition didn't seem to have rekindled it. They weren't kids anymore, he had a family at home, what if anything happened to him? He felt a bit foolish and was less sure than ever this was the best way to pay his respects to Tom. He wondered if the others felt the same way, or did they have a different agenda? Paul was probably trying to eke out his connection with his departed friend a bit longer and Jane had her own reasons, no doubt heavy with history. The news of their brief affair had surprised him, but he wondered if that was what had brought Gwen here or the ghost stories her granddad had told.

Jane made a noise somewhere between surprise and disgust.

"Are you okay?" Martin called.

"Yeah," she said, her voice a bit unsteady.

"Lost cat," said Paul, "but the maggots found it okay."

At Jane's disgusted expression, Gwen turned to see what had happened but had no intention of looking at a dead cat. She was at the Clicking room doors which were unlatched, the gap between them barely noticeable. Gwen cautiously pushed the door nearest her and it opened without protest. She looked at the darkness within, took one last glance back at her old friends who were congregating at the office door and went into the Clicking room.

The space was too large to see the back of, though windows ran around the room just below the ceiling. Those to her right were dark, the ones across from her glowed with pale moonlight. She had no sense of size, her spatial awareness knocked by the darkness and the quiet. The smell of leather was strong and she breathed it in deeply. Stepping forward, she moved her head to describe an arc, wishing her torch beam was more powerful. She picked out a couple of work benches and stepped forward. The one closest to her had a wicker basket on it and three on the floor beside it.

"I'm going on to the next one," said Paul, backing into the corridor.

"Okay," said Jane absently, not taking her eyes off the mess of cat as she stepped over it into the office. Martin watched from the doorway. The office wasn't empty, as he'd thought, but looked like someone had just gone home and never come back. The large desk still had its trays, blotter and piles of paper on it, along with a telephone he'd last seen in an advert with Buzby. Three leather chairs faced the desk and the two windows in the room were covered by venetian blinds. Jane stood in front of a tall filing cabinet, that had a long-dead spider plant trailing from the top.

Martin heard Paul open the next office door and watched him go in. He couldn't see Gwen but the door to the Clicking room was open. He felt something on the back of his neck and rubbed his hand over it quickly, expecting to brush away cobweb but there was nothing there.

Gwen stopped at the first bench. As high as a butchers block and twice as wide, the edges had been scored deeply during its productive life and the smell of leather was very strong, as if it had soaked into the smooth wood. She walked around the bench until she faced the door and peered into the wicker basket but it was empty. She lifted it up, disturbing the dust that covered the basket and the bench top, motes dancing in her torch beam.

She heard something behind her, a gentle click and then a soft voice began to sing.

Lady Bird, Lady Bird,
Fly away home,
Your house is on fire,
Your children will burn

She whirled around, her breath caught in her throat but couldn't see anything other than the next benches.

Martin felt the same sensation, soft and wispy, on the back of his neck and tried to brush it away again but there was nothing there. Irritated, he stepped into the corridor and saw Paul's torch beam shining through the open doorway.

Martin glanced to his left, along the corridor towards the staircase. Somebody was standing in the doorway, only barely visible and he felt a sudden jolt of fear.

The voice sounded distant, certainly not close to Gwen and there was a quality to it, like a small child singing a song it has just learned at school. She turned her head, the torch casting long shadows that didn't illuminate the singer. She took a step further into the room and the singing stopped. There was a sense of movement from far off in the corner to her right though she still couldn't see the wall. She debated heading into the gloom but decided against doing it on her own.

"I want me mammy," said a quiet voice almost at her side, startling her. She gasped and stepped backwards, her hand to her chest. Had she heard it or was it her imagination? She looked around, the beam dancing in the dark but she was alone.

"Shit," she said, "who's there?" Her voice sounded too loud in the silence.

It was a kid, he was sure of it but far enough away the torch beam didn't quite reach. Martin took a cautious step closer, not wanting to spook them.

The kid didn't move. Martin took another step but still the glow didn't quite reach.

"Where are you going?" asked Paul.

"Just down here. Can you see that kid?"

"What kid?"

Martin paused and turned slightly. "The kid at the top of the stairs."

"I can't see anything mate, your imagination is running away with you."

Had he made a mistake? Martin turned back but the shape was still there, only half the height of the doorway. "There," he said, "look."

Paul walked slowly towards him. "I can't see anything, Martin, just the doorway."

"The shape," said Martin, "the fucking person standing there."

Jane pushed the filing cabinet drawer closed. There'd been nothing of interest in there and, as it always did, looking through drawers felt more invasive than wandering around an abandoned space. She heard Martin and Paul talking in the corridor but couldn't catch what they were saying and decided to join them.

She turned slowly, one last scan of the room to make sure she hadn't missed anything and watched her torch beam cast shadows that moved across the floor and wall.

The person sitting behind the desk startled her.

The voice hadn't spoken again, though Gwen listened intently for it. Now she could hear Martin and Paul talking in the corridor and decided it might be better to stick with them.

She slowly backed away until the side of a bench dug into her left buttock. From the corner of her eye she saw movement, a shadow coming towards her.

"Martin?" she said. The person didn't answer but moved across the doorway, the faint light from the corridor silhouetting them. "Martin?"

The figure came at her quickly without saying anything. She felt sharp needles of panic at her wrists and her chest was tight. She stepped back, reaching behind to check for obstructions. Her pace matched the figures but she was moving into an area she hadn't been before and that scared her.

"Paul?" she called, "stop it, this is silly."

The figure didn't respond and Gwen realised she couldn't hear footsteps on the wooden floor. As she passed the next bench she moved to her right, not taking her eyes off the person. She moved further, aiming to keep at least half the bench between them though she wanted them to move into her torch beam so she could see who she was dealing with. The shape, broadly, was right for both of her old friends but why would they do this to her?

When the person reached the bench, she could barely draw breath she was so scared. Her head felt odd, foggy and sharp at the same time and she bit her lip, focussing on them, willing them to come into the light.

Another step closer. She wanted to move, every ounce

of her was screaming too but she needed to stay still for one more moment, one more step.

"Martin?" she ventured. "Paul?"

The person moved into the shallow edge of light but Gwen couldn't see a face.

Jane screamed.

Martin grabbed Paul's arm and pulled him towards the office. Jane was in the doorway, breathing heavily.

"What is it?"

"In there," she gasped, "there's somebody at the desk."

"What?" asked Paul. "I didn't see anybody."

He rushed into the office, Martin right behind him.

Gwen backed around the bench. "Who are you?"

The person raised their right arm and she could see something hanging from it. Was it a belt? Was this person going to attack her? She backed away, the person advancing quicker. Stumbling, she managed to keep to her feet and then realised she was past the bench.

"Martin!" she yelled, "help me!"

"There's nobody in here," said Paul, standing just beyond the door. Martin poked his head around and there was clearly no-one else in the room.

"There is, behind the desk," said Jane, "I bloody saw them."

"The chair is empty," Paul said.

From the Clicking room, Martin heard Gwen shout his name. He rushed across the corridor, Jane just behind him.

Gwen backed away, cowering slightly, one arm raised

in front of her, the other feeling desperately behind her in case she walked into anything. The person kept coming and the belt whipped down, slicing the air and hitting the floor in front of her. Dust danced in her torch beam.

"Martin!"

She stumbled again, falling back and the belt whipped at the floor twice. She scuttled backwards, turned, got to her feet and ran. The torch beam bobbed and cast too many shadows for her to properly see but for now she didn't care, she just had to get away.

She passed more benches, what looked like a press and a stack of wicker baskets. Someone called her name.

Then the floor wasn't there anymore and she was falling.

Chapter 9

Martin crossed the corridor in a few strides and ran into the Clicking room. He could see the glow of Gwen's torch dancing crazily over obstructions and moved sideways, trying to get a clear sight beyond a row of benches.

Paul was behind him. "Where is she?"

"Down there somewhere."

"What's happening?" Jane asked.

Martin stopped. He could see Gwen. She was on her backside pushing herself further in the darkness. She turned, got unsteadily to her feet and ran.

"Gwen!" he called.

She kept running and didn't turn, then she wasn't there anymore. She screamed and he heard a terribly heavy thud.

"Fuck," he said and ran.

"Where did she go?" asked Paul, running alongside him.

They passed more benches, running into a narrow channel formed by what looked like presses. Visibility was difficult as their torches made haphazard shadows dance around them but all too quickly it was clear where she had gone.

Martin slowed, edging around the hole. The floorboards had snapped, the exposed edges lined with lethal looking splinters, several of which were red at the tip. Testing the boards nearest to the edge, he knelt down and looked over.

She'd fallen into the room below, his torch beam only vaguely making out her shape. Her own torch was some way off.

"Gwen? Gwen? Are you okay?" She made a noise that could have meant anything. "We'll be right down."

Paul knelt on the other side of the hole. "Can you see her?"

"Not clearly. What's down there, the rough cutting room?"

Paul looked up and around. "Yeah, I think so."

Jane ran up and both men called her name, making her slow to a trot. "Holy shit," she said, when she saw the hole.

"So we go back the way we came," said Martin.

"Yes," said Paul.

"Is she okay?" asked Jane.

"Can't tell," said Martin.

Paul led them out of the Clicking room, along the corridor and down the stairs. Martin briefly thought of the shape he'd seen but pushed it to the back of his mind, now wasn't the time to worry about that.

They retraced their footprints in the dust of the reception area and into the corridor. Paul pulled open the rough cutting room door. "We'll spread out, Jane through the middle, me on the left. When you find her, shout and we'll meet up."

The room felt heavy and crowded, though Martin couldn't see far. Metal beams crossed the low ceiling and light fixtures hung down, coated with dark webs. He looked at Jane, seeing her torch beam pick out the edge of a large press. He went to his right, close to the wall until he reached the end of the machine then headed through the canyon formed with the next press. He kept his gaze down, the moonlight that filtered through the windows not reaching the gritty floor.

"Gwen!" he heard Paul shout. There was no answer.

At the edge of the press, the room opened up and the centre space, as far as he could see, was dominated by long benches. Jane was to his left, walking between the benches looking down.

"Gwen!" Paul again. Martin bit his lip and kept moving forward, the longer they waited to find her, surely, the worse it would be.

"Here!" shouted Jane, "I've found her."

Martin ran, cutting behind another bench and reaching Jane as Paul did. She was crying, the tear tracks on her cheeks glistening in the torch light.

"Is she...?" asked Paul.

"Of course not, you can hear her," said Jane.

Gwen was breathing steadily but it was a terrible wheezing sound. She'd landed on her back on one of the benches, her left arm hanging uselessly over the side with an unnatural bump at her shoulder. Her left leg looked fine, her right leg was folded back on itself at the knee. Martin looked away, fighting the urge to retch.

"Fuck," Paul said.

Martin looked at the ceiling as he took his phone out of his pocket. There was no signal. "We need to get help."

"No signal," Paul said when he checked. "I'll go outside and call someone, you two stay here and do what you can."

"What can we do?" asked Jane. "I daren't move her."

"No," said Martin, "we can't move her."

Paul made a frustrated sound deep in his throat. "I don't know what to do," he said finally. "I'll go and call for help."

Jane watched him go, shaking her head. "It's been years since I did any First Aid."

"I can't remember when I did it," Martin said, "so I'll bow to your superior knowledge."

"I don't know what it'd do to fall this far but it can't be good. Her left arm is dislocated, if not broken and her right leg is a mess. Judging by her breathing, she might have broken ribs pushing into her lungs."

Martin still daren't look at Gwen. "Her spine must be damaged, surely? What about her skull?" He took out his mobile and activated the torch on it, shining it around her head. Her hair was fanned out on the bench, strands of it over her face, but he couldn't see any blood.

"There could be fractures," Jane said and took a deep breath. "Jesus, this is fucking shitty. I just wish I knew how to do more."

"You're doing a grand job," Martin said and looked up, directing his phone at the ceiling. The hole was about three feet wide and maybe twice as long. Bits of floorboard were littered across the floor at his feet and over the benches beside him. "I don't get why the floor gave way though."

"It's an old building, maybe it had woodworm."

"Maybe. But what was she doing, why was she running further into the Clicking room? We couldn't see anything with the torch beams going everywhere."

"I was too far back, I couldn't even see her."

"She was on her backside, looking up at something and then turned and ran."

"And you didn't see anything?"

"Not a thing."

Jane looked at him, pushing her bump cap up so the

light didn't catch his eyes. "What's going on, Martin?"

"What do you mean?"

"We're in an abandoned building and the person who told us she'd heard ghost stories about the place falls through a floor after running away from something none of us could see."

"Maybe she got spooked."

"But she's done this before." She bit her lip. "What about what I saw? There was nobody in that room when I went in but I'd fucking swear I saw someone behind the desk."

"Did you see them clearly?"

"No, it was just a shadow, a darker spot against the wall."

"Do you think you saw a ghost?"

"I saw something," she said and looked away. "I don't know."

Martin looked at the ceiling again. "I saw something too," he said, after a moment.

"What?"

He told her what he'd seen in the corridor, making sure to mention that Paul hadn't seen it. "Could it be suggestion? We're in an old factory, we've heard ghost stories, we're putting two and two together and making eight?"

Gwen moved her head slightly and let out a long moan.

"Gwen?" said Jane, leaning close.

"Fell," she said, the word falling between the wheezes of her breath.

"Yes, you fell a bit. But we're with you and Paul's gone to ring for help."

"Fell."

"Yes, I know."

"Where's he...?"

"Who?"

"He."

"I don't..."

"Did you see someone Gwen?" asked Martin but she coughed, her face contorting in pain.

"Try not to move," said Jane.

The floorboards creaked and Martin looked up. "Did you hear that?"

"No."

He heard footsteps and looked up as a light appeared between two of the presses. "Paul?"

"Yeah, couldn't get the fucking door open."

"So you haven't rung?"

"I couldn't get out," he said, coming to stand at the end of the bench. He looked at Gwen, then at Jane. "You need to come with me mate, we'll get the door open together then I can ring."

Gwen coughed and blood flecked her lips and chin.

"Shit," said Jane.

"We need to go," said Martin.

Gwent began to wheeze, her lips pulling tight with pain. There was blood on her teeth.

"What's happening?" yelled Paul. "What's going on?"

"It's her lungs," said Jane.

"What?"

She held up her hands. "Quiet, I'm trying to remember. It's pulmonary something, you bruise the lungs and blood can gather. If she fell onto her back, there's all manner of things."

"But we need to sort it quick?"

Gwen coughed, whimpered and her wheezing began to slow.

"Yes," said Jane, "very quick."

Gwen coughed once more. Martin waited for the following wheeze but it didn't come. He looked at Jane, who put her fingers against Gwen's neck.

"I can't find a pulse," she said after a while, her eyes shining with tears.

"She's not breathing," Martin said.

"This can't be happening," said Paul, "this is just bloody stupid."

"There's somebody there," said Jane, her voice calm and low.

It took Martin a moment to process her words and he looked towards the door, where a shape stood in the darkness.

"What?" asked Paul.

"In the doorway we came through, somebody's watching us."

"Maybe they can help," said Paul.

Martin squinted, the constant movement of the torches playing havoc with his vision. "Is it a kid?"

"I don't know," Jane said, still subdued, "I can't see properly."

"Didn't you say you saw a kid before?" demanded Paul.

"I thought so."

"Right, well if he's running around in here, he might know what's going on."

"What do you mean?" said Jane.

"I mean I'm going to have a word." Without waiting for them to say anything, Paul ran across the room. As his torch beam bounced off the wall, Martin could see the doorway was empty.

"What do we do?" asked Jane. "I don't want to leave Gwen alone."

"No, but we don't want to get split up either."

"Should we go after him?"

"Yeah, especially if there is a kid there."

"Okay," said Jane and put her hand on Gwen's forehead. "We'll be back soon for you."

With a quick glance left to make sure nobody was by the jammed-closed door, Paul ran along the corridor, his beam dancing across the walls and floor. The reception door was closed and he had a moment of panic, wondering if the kid had ducked into the changing room but kept moving.

He hit the door without pausing and it swung wide, banging off the wall. The dust on the reception floor was so disturbed it was impossible to tell if anyone other than them had been through here. He ran to the other door, pulled it open and went up the stairs two at a time. On the landing, he paused to get his breath back, straining for a sound that might give the intruder away.

Other than himself, he couldn't hear anything.

"Where are you?" he said quietly. He walked up the corridor, training the torch beam on the floor to see where the dust was disturbed. He passed the Clicking room and the office Jane had investigated. Beyond that, the dust was undisturbed. He turned and saw lights in the stairwell and felt a quick jolt of fear in his chest before realising it was Martin and Jane coming after him.

They walked briskly up the corridor to him. "Did you see anyone?" asked Martin.

"No, not a soul. They must still be downstairs."

"They can only be in the changing room," said Jane.

"Let's head back and take a look. I don't want to be in here any longer."

The office door slammed shut and Paul felt something brush past him. He turned, caught the vaguest glimpse of movement and then it was gone. Jane squealed, turning and grabbing for fresh air.

"In the Clicking room," she said and ran across the corridor. He stayed close behind her and the door slammed shut as soon as he was through it, leaving Martin in the corridor.

Chapter 10

Jane rounded on him. "Why did you shut the door?" she demanded.

"I didn't," Paul said, painfully aware of the whine in his voice. Why did she bring this side out in him? "The door shut on its own."

"Well open it, let him in."

Paul tried the handle but the door didn't move. "It's stuck," he said weakly.

"You're a fucking idiot, let me do it."

She elbowed him out of the way and rattled the door back and forth. He hadn't heard it lock but it was closed fast.

With a frustrated growl, she let go and paced away, then turned. "What's going on, Paul?"

"What? I know as much as you do."

She stepped towards him, her face drawn, her lips a tight line. He watched her, vaguely frightened of what she might do. She took a breath, looked as if she was going to say something and then shook her head.

"What?"

"Don't," she said and held up a finger. "Seriously. I don't know what's going on and I don't understand any of it except Gwen is hurt badly and we need to call the ambulance."

"Yes."

"We have to find a way out. Everything else, all this other shit I'm sure you understand better than I do, we can deal with that later."

"What shit?"

She held up her finger again and bit her lip. "Don't," she said and turned.

Paul looked at her back, then at the door. They weren't going through there, that much was certain. He shrugged off his backpack and took out the walkie talkie. "Martin? Can you hear me?" There was a squelch of static but nothing else. "Martin? Are you there?" He put the unit in his pocket, hoping Martin had the good sense to head downstairs and try to get out.

Jane had walked away, keeping close to the wall.

"Where are you going?"

"To find a way out," she called over her shoulder. "I don't intend to spend all night in here and I want to make sure Martin's alright."

"Why wouldn't he be?"

She didn't reply but kept walking.

Jane didn't have a plan but had to get away from Paul for a few minutes otherwise she'd slap his smug face. There was too much going that she had no explanation for but something about him, his attitude and responses, screamed out to her that he did know something.

She walked slowly, keeping as close to the wall as possible, fear tingling through her arms and fingers. She thought of Gwen, poor Gwen, on that bench downstairs and fresh tears filled her eyes. She blinked them away, better to see the floor and make sure none of the boards were rotten.

She passed little stands, small tables and racks, edging around larger objects and concentrating hard, trying not to think about what had happened. She just hoped there was an entrance on the other side of the room, the darkness seemed to be pressing against her and she didn't like it.

"Jane?"

He sounded whiny, which made her even more mad at him. He wasn't a fortysomething bloke anymore but a petulant teenager who wasn't getting his own way. She could feel the annoyance building in her, pushing back the fear.

"Jane?"

"What?" She stopped and turned carefully. He was coming towards her, his measured pace slowing under her glare.

"How do you know the exit's this way?"

"I don't, because some dickhead didn't get a floor plan." He flinched but didn't say anything and that made her feel better. There were still threads of fear, lingering in her belly, but she could deal with them. "If there's only one way out then we're knackered."

"Agreed," he said, contrition clear in his voice. "In theory, there should be access between here and downstairs, perhaps upstairs as well."

They looked at one another and she realised that fighting was silly, it wasn't about him and her, it was trying to find Martin and getting someone for Gwen. "Well," she said, "what're you waiting for?"

He nodded and caught up with her and they fell into step together, Jane keeping close to the wall though she noticed his light was trained on the floor too.

"I didn't know any of this was going to happen," he said after a while.

"I know."

"But you said..."

"I know what I said, Paul, but I was scared and angry

- I'm still angry - and when that happens I say things I normally wouldn't."

"I understand," he said. "You don't like me much, do you?"

"Not at the moment."

"I don't think you ever have."

"Oh piss off, Paul, now isn't the time to garner sympathy."

"I mean it."

She stopped and looked at him. "I'm here because I wanted to be, to pay my respects to someone I once knew. That's the truth and I'm grateful you organised it."

"Did you love him?"

Did she really want to be having this conversation right now, with him? "What kind of question is that?"

"Just a question."

"So did you?"

"What do you mean?"

"I mean that if there was anyone who didn't like someone else, it was you over me. As soon as Tom and I got together, that's when things changed."

"You're mad."

"No I'm not, I knew it then and I know it now. Did you ever tell him you were gay for him?"

"Oh fuck off Jane."

"I'd love to, but were you?"

"No, I fucking wasn't."

"You were never jealous of me?"

"No, of course not."

"Not that I was taking up his time?"

"No."

"Not that he was paying less attention to you."

"We were good friends," he said, with an edge in his

voice, "and that's how we stayed until he passed away."

She took a deep breath. "He used people Paul, it was his way of doing things. He figured out what he wanted, laid on the charm and when he had his fill, moved on."

"That's bollocks."

She smiled tightly at him. "You think?"

"I know."

Jane started to walk again, her head down. She could hear occasional clicks from the gloom of the room, as the factory settled around them. "How often did he keep in touch between coming back here?"

Beside her, Paul shook his head. "He wasn't a Facebook kind of bloke, you know that."

"I'm not a Facebook kind of girl but there are other ways to keep in touch."

He didn't say anything as they reached the corner. On the wall was a large poster extolling safety at work and someone had written over it in marker pen, adding dialogue, facial hair and glasses to the figures on it. Below the poster was a sink and under that a wicker basket that was overflowing with scraps of fabric stained a deep red.

"This must be where the corridor turns," said Paul, "so there should be a doorway somewhere along this wall."

"Why?"

"Because those windows over there," he pointed across the room, "are the back of the factory."

Pausing made the darkness seem to creep around her and she felt the tingles in her arm and fingers again. "Let's keep moving," she said briskly.

They walked in silence for a few paces. "He wasn't really a bastard, you know."

Mark West

"Maybe not to you, but he was to me."

"It was a long time ago, Jane."

"And sometimes, pain gets lodged so deep it takes a long while to edge its way out."

It was harder for Jane to stay close to the wall as there was more equipment now, on narrow benches set out at intervals. The smell of leather was stronger and she could see off-cuts of it, stacked in small piles against the skirting board.

"There's something up ahead," he said after a while.

Leaning to her right to see around his shoulder, she saw a faint reflection of light ahead, as if their torches were catching a piece of glass.

"It could be another picture at the corner," she said. There was a sound behind her and she turned. "Did you hear that?"

"What?"

What was it, a sigh perhaps or movement because it certainly wasn't the building settling. Fear flared in her belly. Why was she so spooked? "Nothing," she said, "keep going." She followed him, trying to force down the sensations of being frightened as they threatened to bubble over. She needed to keep a clear head but the darkness was pressing against her and she could almost feel the shift in the air as people moved just past the edge of her vision.

Sound drifted to them, as if from the other side of the Clicking room and Paul stopped, holding his right hand up. Jane felt her shoulders pull tight as disquiet wrapped her in a chill blanket.

"Can you hear that?" he whispered.

"Yes," she said quietly, her voice sounding far too tiny. "It sounds like singing, but it's too soft, I can't hear

86

it properly."

"Is it kids?"

"I don't know."

"It must be outside."

Jane turned slowly, both wanting and not wanting to see anything. She held her breath and bit her lip - if she saw someone in the gloom, she knew she'd scream - but her torch beam illuminated nothing.

"No," she said, shaking her head quickly and suddenly sure, "it's in here."

"It could be the kid we followed upstairs?"

She felt the skin on her arm crawl. "Maybe they're hiding in here, watching us and one of their phones is going off."

"There's no signal."

"Not for us."

The singing had grown louder as they talked and Jane could now make out the words.

There was an Old Woman,
Liv'd under a Hill,
And if she 'int gone,
She lives there still.

The sound played up and down her spine with cold fingers. "That's a nursery rhyme."

"Why would someone be playing that?"

"I don't think they are," she said, "I think it's kids singing."

"Must be outside."

"It isn't, you said it yourself, we're at the back of the factory."

There was a loud thump, as if someone had run into a

wall, the sound loud enough to make her shriek.

"What was that?" Paul said quickly.

Jane pressed her hand to her chest and felt her heart thudding. "Behind me," she said.

He looked at her and when his expression didn't change, she glanced behind.

"What the fuck?" The sense of unease she'd been feeling grew. The man behind the desk, the kid in the doorway, was it really someone else in here? Or was it something else altogether, something that she wasn't prepared to even admit, much less vocalise to him.

"Quick," he hissed, "we need to move."

"What? Why?"

He reached for her hand but she shook his grip off. "Jane, come on."

The singing got louder and, just beyond the reach of her torch beam, she was aware of movement in the shadows. "What is that?"

He walked away. Surprised, she followed him, keeping as close to the wall as the benches would allow. "What're you doing?"

"I'll explain in a minute."

The singing grew in volume but was dropping behind, as if they were walking away from the choir. Ahead, the reflective surface flashed their lights back at them.

"It's a door," he said, glancing over his shoulder.

"Are we running away from something?"

He was looking ahead so she kept her light trained on the floor. There were more noises behind her, shuffling and bumps and she tried to shut them out, listening instead to the rhythm of her pulse, feeling the thud of her heartbeat increasing in her chest and throat.

They reached the door and Paul pressed the handle

down as if expecting it to be locked. It wasn't and moved easily. He pulled it open and looked at her, his eyes wide.

"What?" she asked, "what?"

Grabbing her shoulder, he pushed her through the door. As she went, she glanced back and saw, for the briefest of moments, someone on the floor. Almost bleached out in the torchlight, they were dragging themselves along on their elbows, their legs useless behind them.

She screamed and stumbled, her foot catching on a floorboard. She felt, then heard, something click and her left ankle exploded in pain. She cried out and fell onto her side.

Paul slammed the door shut and grimaced when something thumped against it. Jane was on the floor, her face a mask of pain and he knelt beside her.

"What've you done?"

It took her a moment or two to reply and he looked at her legs, trying to find some kind of visible injury.

"My ankle," she hissed, "I've twisted it."

He couldn't see any swelling but didn't know what a broken ankle looked like. "Can you get up?"

"I don't know." He held out his hand and she grabbed it, pulling herself to her knees, then holding his shoulder to stand up. As soon as she put pressure on her leg, he didn't need to hear her cry out because the pain was clear to see in her face. Whatever was behind the door thumped it again, as if in sympathy.

"What was that?"

"I'm not sure. Come on, we need to get you out of here."

"How, are you going to carry me?"

"Yeah, no." He paused. "Hold on."

They were on a long, wide landing. A staircase went down a few feet beyond where they stood and another went up to their right, far enough away it was only just visible in the torch beams. Across the landing were two unmarked offices, one with the door closed and a hole above the kick plate, the other with the door ajar.

Paul looked at the Clicking room door and then the down staircase.

"If we put you in that office, I'll head downstairs and see if there's an exit."

"What?"

"I can get downstairs quicker on my own."

"You'll leave me," she cried, her voice rising.

"I won't, I promise. I'll check what's down there and if there's any way out I'll come back."

She didn't say anything, just looked at him with wide eyes. He looked around the landing but couldn't see another option. "Come on." She put her arm over his shoulder and, slowly, they made their way to the office with its door ajar.

A quick glance around proved it hadn't been used in a long time. Dust was thick on the floor and across the surface of a wooden desk in the corner, the only furniture. A narrow window was high up on the far wall and there was a small hatch in the floor to the right of the desk.

"Are you okay?" Grimacing, she nodded her head as he set her down on the floor by the door. "Yell if you need me, I'll be back as soon as I can."

She held his hand. "Don't fucking leave me."

"I won't," he said and meant it.

Chapter 11

The door slammed shut and Martin grabbed for the handle. It turned and he pulled at it angrily but the door steadfastly stayed closed.

"Paul, open the door!"

He didn't hear a response if there was one. Taking a deep breath, Martin turned so he had his back to the door. He looked across the corridor towards the office Jane had been exploring and then to his right, where the end of the corridor was lost in shadow.

"Fuck it," he said and began down the corridor towards the reception staircase. He didn't know why Paul had shut the door but he had to try and get in touch with the police. He thought of how poor Gwen had looked and felt nausea rise - how could that have happened? What was she running from? How could an evening that had started out as a silly, if well-intentioned, brush with nostalgia resulted in the death of an old friend? And what about the kid they'd seen, or the one he'd seen earlier or the person Jane saw?

Martin was a realist, he didn't believe in ghosts but suddenly felt uncomfortable, as if the darkness in the corridor was suddenly alive, crowding him. He could feel the beginnings of the headaches he suffered at the base of his skull - stress-aches, Ellen called them.

He remembered the walkie-talkie and dug it out of the backpack. Compact and basic, it didn't take long to figure out how it worked. "Paul? Are you there, can you hear this? I don't know why you shut the door on me but I'm making my way down to the entrance. If you can hear this, I suggest you do the same."

His skin suddenly felt tight across his shoulders and there was a sense he wasn't alone. He glanced over his shoulder, hoping to see his friends but the corridor was empty. He put the walkie-talkie in his pocket and pulled out his mobile, just in case he needed the flashlight.

There had to be a rational explanation, didn't there? He was a photographer, a family man who lived in London and went to friends houses for dinner and took his girls to the park and pushed them high on the swings until, giggling, they begged him to stop. From the viewpoint of that life, this line of thinking was ridiculous. That life was a wide street outside his front door, sun in his garden, the noise of the girls playing, the look of his wife as she stretched, waking up in the morning with sunlight creeping through the curtains. But that life wasn't here, in a dark corridor with one friend lying downstairs and two others locked in a room. That life wasn't seeing things through the pale glow of a headtorch and rarely felt lonely - right now, it seemed like he was the last man on earth and the space around him was shrinking. He recognised this feeling of claustrophobia, from explorations in the past when corridors had ended abruptly or passages had turned too narrow to continue and knew he had to ride it out. In an old building, panicking at claustrophobia was a sure way to get yourself into trouble.

He was scared.

"Get a grip," he said, his voice louder than he'd expected.

From behind him came a soft sobbing.

He felt a surge of fear run through him, hot at his

pulse points, cold down his back. The pain in the base of his skull suddenly amplified and he could hear his own heartbeat. He closed his eyes and dropped his head, not sure of what to do next.

"I want me mammy," said a quiet voice, a lot closer than the sob had sounded. Startled, he turned and held his phone up. Nothing. There was a sense of movement, just where the light faded to darkness and he took a couple of steps forward but still nothing - if anyone was there, they were retreating as he advanced.

"Who's there?"

"Mister, will you help us?"

The voice was behind him, from the side, from all around. He whirled in a circle, the torch beam and flashlight app only showing the empty corridor. The lights cast quick, shifting shadows from door frames that disappeared almost as quickly.

He was alone in the corridor, he was convinced of it.

"Mister, please?"

The voice was to his left. "Who's there?"

"Mister?" the voice was louder, sharper, as if pleased it had finally found someone.

"Who are you?" he asked, slowly walking up the corridor towards the Clicking room door.

"Please mister, will you help us?"

Each time they spoke gave him a location to aim at and he was drawn towards the office where Jane had seen the person. The voice he could hear sounded like a child, but she hadn't specified that. Could someone have broken in here to mess around with them? As much as he didn't want it to, that sounded so irrational as to be ridiculous - who would know they'd be in here, for a start. But then, he thought, suddenly feeling a quick and cold caress over his shoulders, what else did that leave?

"Mister?"

Martin moved to the side of the corridor, keeping close to the wall and could now see the open doorway of the office. Another four or five paces and he'd be there. Then what? Did he burst in, or go in slowly? If there was a kid in there, what would he do? If it was someone playing a trick on him, would they be expecting him - after all, he hadn't been quiet (none of them had) and he still had the torch and light on. But if the office was empty, then what?

Fear rippled across his scalp, tightening the skin as it went. What would he do if it was empty?

He reached the office. The door opened to his right so he couldn't see the interior without going in. He took a deep breath.

"Please mister, I want me mammy."

The voice was of a little kid, so close it felt like they were standing beside him and he thought of the girls, the way they'd reach for his hand as they walked, talking ten-to-the-dozen and assuming he not only understood their conversation topics but had his own opinions on them. Without thinking, he looked down.

"Where is she?" he asked, his voice low and quiet.

"I don't know," said the voice plaintively.

"Are you hurt?" The silence that followed seemed to last for ages. He was holding his breath, feeling the pressure in his chest. A steady ticking sound came from somewhere, like water dripping and the occasional knock as if the wind was blowing against a tile.

"No," the voice said finally.

Martin held his phone up, shining the light into the room. It caught the filing cabinet, filling half the wall behind it in deep shadow. "Can you see my light?"

"No," the voice said without hesitation.

"But you can hear me?"

"Oh yes."

Martin stepped over the threshold. He'd expected to feel something, a drop in temperature perhaps or the sensation he was sharing space with someone else but didn't. Careful not to nudge the door, he took another step but then his feet refused to take the final step, that would see him in the office properly. His heart rate was increasing, his palms sweaty, his lips dry. Just one more step.

A floor tile creaked behind him and he turned quickly.

"Help me."

Another illusion. Martin took a deep breath and went into the office, moving his head quickly and holding the phone at chest height, panning it across the empty desk. It was coated in a layer of dust. The pinboard on the wall behind the desk had several yellowing sheets of paper showing figures and charts on it and they moved slightly with a breeze.

"Where are you?" he asked, checking behind the filing cabinet.

No-one answered. He rolled his head on his shoulders and rubbed his neck. The stress-ache was pounding harder now, fingers of it creeping across his forehead. He'd expected to find something in here, but wasn't sure if finding it empty was a good or bad sign. Had he really heard something or was it just his imagination? That made more sense, surely.

"You idiot," he said, thinking of Gwen downstairs. All that mattered was making that call. He went out into the corridor and tried the Clicking room door again but it was still closed. Shaking his head, he rushed towards the staircase and was at the top when he heard children singing.

Sing a Song of Sixpence,
A bag full of Rye,
Four and twenty
Naughty boys,
Bak'd in a Pye.

Their voices were scratchy and off-key and he felt the tune drag up his spine. Fear rushed through him and he felt the corridor walls close in, the darkness pressing against the two torch beams.

"Who's there?" he called. "This isn't funny."

The singers began a new song.

Lady Bird, Lady Bird,
Fly away home,
Your house is on fire,
Your children will burn

He knew he had to go downstairs but those kids, the singing, he had to know. Holding his phone in front of him to keep as wide an area illuminated as possible he turned and walked back along the corridor. The children sang the sixpence song, their voices now mournful and downcast, as if being forced to sing rather than doing it for the joy of the activity.

He passed the Clicking room door and the office, following the voices, his torch beams pushing the darkness back as he went. He liked that. Moving helped too, dispelling the illusion the walls were encroaching. As he didn't know how long the corridor was he couldn't work out how far the sound was carrying but it sounded, tantalisingly, as if it was just hidden beyond the fringe of black in front of him. He was convinced that, at any moment, he would see a small group of children standing in the middle of the corridor, songbooks held in front of them, like a Christmas card image of choristers.

His lights reflected back and he paused, squinting. He'd reached the end of the corridor and a large painting of a horse was hung on the wall, the glass of it dusty and smudged. The corridor continued to the right and he peered around the corner but only saw more of the same - it stretched beyond the limit of his lights and there were a lot of office doors.

Martin kept walking. The outer wall, to his left, was blank with no windows or pictures. After a hundred yards or so, he came to another corner and followed it. The corridor stretched into darkness again and he tried to get his bearings. Surely, now, he was at the back of the factory?

He walked until something flashed ahead of him and he slowed, moving the phone until he saw the flash again. When he reached it, he saw it was a large painting of a horse, the glass dusty and smudged. He looked behind him and then peered around the corner. More offices on the right, blank wall to the left.

There was something terribly wrong here. He slipped off his backpack and fished out the stick of chalk Paul had given them what felt like hours ago. Kneeling, he chalked a large X onto the wallpaper below the painting, pocketed the chalk and started walking.

He listened to the children, their voices loud in the corridor. His heartbeat was still quick and he matched his stride to his pulse. The corridor, as he'd expected, ended with a blank wall and he followed it around. His chest felt tight and his stress-ache pounded, as if someone was hitting the top of his bump cap with a rubber mallet.

He was waiting for the flash, every ounce of his being focussed on it. He walked, slowing without realising he was doing so. More doors, indistinct now, each as bland as the other, nothing more than decoration to pass the time. Another step, another day, another round of Lady Bird, Lady Bird.

When he saw the flash he stopped, his breath hard to find. It was impossible, he knew it. He walked, slowly now, until his lights showed him the wallpaper under the painting and the chalk X he'd drawn. It was smudged, as if small hands had tried to brush it off, but it was very definitely there.

He leaned against the wall, hands on his knees, trying to draw a deep breath. How could this be, what kind of bizarre geometry made this possible? It made no sense to go on but then, it made no real sense to go back either. How many more corners did he have to turn to get back to the original corridor, the one where the Clicking room was? Was he trapped in this insanity? He could feel the claustrophobia weighing heavily on him, pressing against his lungs, making his breathing choppy and shallow. He held his phone up, shining it on the opposite wall, wanting to keep it at bay.

"Help me, mister." His head turned, the light catching only a sensation of movement in the darkness. This time, he wasn't going to let them go and ran down the corridor, holding the phone out, the torch on his cap bouncing and throwing disorientating shadows across the walls and ceiling. He could see a shape in the gloom and ran faster, trying to keep up.

The shape disappeared.

Martin slowed to a halt, shining his torch against the doors. They were all the same, two panels and no glass. He checked the floor to see if the dust had been disturbed but the footprints appeared to be his, going the other way.

He pointed his phone along the corridor, trying to gauge where the light didn't penetrate the darkness. He estimated the difference and thought it might be a dozen or so paces, which meant the person must have ducked into a door that much further away.

He walked, checking the doors and the floor, counting his steps. The children had stopped singing now and he wondered if that was because he'd seen one of them, however vaguely.

When he got to twelve, he stopped and looked at the door. Words had been scratched into the lock rail panel and he angled his phone so the torch beam highlighted them.

"Don't feed the beast," he read.

He tried the handle and it moved easily, so he pushed the door open. It went without a sound and he smelled leather and, below it, a metallic tang.

"Is someone in here?" he asked, trying to keep his voice steady.

The silence felt oppressive.

"I saw you come in. Who are you?"

The silence seemed to conspire with the darkness, to coddle itself around him.

"Were you the one who asked me to help before?"

As he expected, there was no answer. He stepped forward, his free hand on the door, holding his breath, ready for anything. "Why are you hiding?" His voice seemed to echo.

He let go of the door, moving further into the room. It was square, the side walls plastered, the lower halves dark green, the upper halves beige. Paint of both colours was peeling off. The wall across from him was bare brick with a square hole on the far side, blood-stained teeth crudely painted around it. A three-legged table was propped against the wall to his right and there were three wicker baskets in the corner to his left.

Keeping his back to the wall, Martin edged to the baskets. Two were empty, the last was filled with crusty wads of fabric stained a deep red. From this vantage point, he could see the corridor wall was painted the same as the sides, peeling as much as they were. There were no pictures or charts, no sign this had been an office of any kind apart from the table. There was also no place to hide, unless the person had climbed into the hole on the wall? And was that the beast the writing on the door warned of?

He had to look into that hole, to make sure it was empty.

Keeping his eye on the doorway, he edged along the wall, running his hand over the bare brick behind him. When he reached the hole, he turned to face it.

The teeth had been drawn on with chalk, the blood dark and thick and bitty. He held his phone close to it but didn't want to believe he was looking at the real thing. More red was smeared at the sides of the hole and he held the phone into it. The darkness parted to reveal a narrow brick channel that angled downwards, some kind of chute to a lower part of the factory.

There was a flurry of noise from the doorway and something knocked his arm. He dropped the phone and it clattered into the hole, disappearing from sight.

"Shit!"

He turned but saw no-one. Fear fogged him, his head ached like it was in a vice and his breath caught in his throat. He tried to move towards the door but was bumped again and staggered sideways, hitting the table which slid down the wall. He almost fell himself but managed to stay on his feet.

He pressed against the wall and felt small hands on his side. They pushed him and, surprised, he took a step sideways to keep himself upright. The hands pushed again, pressing into his belly and upper legs. He reached out his right arm to steady himself but where they should have hit brick there was nothing.

Scared, he flailed wildly, desperate to grab the wall. He turned, saw he was in front of the hole and the brickwork pressed against his upper legs. He felt his centre of balance shift and tried to throw himself sideways but the hands kept pushing. With a cry, he was over the edge.

Martin landed heavily, expecting the floor of the channel to be rough but the bricks were worn smooth. He spread his legs, digging his toes into the walls, trying to catch any kind of outcrop that could slow his descent. His left arm was under his body, his right pushed out ahead. He struggled to keep his head up, the top of his bump cap brushing brick. The channel angled down, speeding his descent and he pressed his knees against the walls as best he could. The pads danced against his legs but did slow him a little. His torch beam danced, the repetition of brickwork disorientating. Bits of grit sprayed his face and he squinted against them.

The channel narrowed, pushing his head down. His

chin grazed brick, making him cry out. His knees were pushed in and the bricks battered his toes. He pressed his hands down but they didn't slow him and skin peeled from his palms.

The walls pressed his shoulders, pushing his head down and he tilted it sideways, to protect his chin. The bump cap slipped on his head, catching the brick and that scared him - no hat meant no light.

He pushed his head up, the bump cap jerking and tugging his neck. The channel grew narrower, his legs pushing in until, with a jolt, he stopped. The sudden halt whipped his head forward and the cap slid off. With a scream, he grabbed for it and caught the brim, the torch shining into his face.

He was wedged tight, unable to move but at least he still had light.

Gravity pulled at the cap and although he moved his hand to get a better grip he felt the brim slide between his finger and thumb. The torch beam moved sideways as the hat slipped from his grasp and he watched it go, bouncing over and over until it dropped out of sight.

He was in darkness.

Chapter 12

The stairwell was wide with shallow steps marked at their edges by metal strips. A banister ran down either side and framed pictures - views of Gaffney, the factory, members of the workforce - were placed intermittently above them.

Behind Paul, the landing was lit by the weak glow of Jane's torch. It was moving, as if she was checking out the office. Things had taken a very odd turn, one he'd been aware of but was convinced wouldn't happen.

It seemed as if Tom was right.

The bottom of the stairwell was hidden in gloom. He kept walking, training his torch light on the steps. They all seemed intact and dusty and he wondered where Tom had been, as his footprints should have been visible.

Paul came to a small, square landing, walls on three sides. The facing wall had a Health & Safety poster on it, the wall to his left was blank and the one to his right had 'Fear The Beast' spray-painted in red. The paint had run on some of the letters and looked as though it had been on the wall for a long time.

"Fuck," he said, his voice loud in the space. Why would a staircase led nowhere, it didn't make sense. He looked up the stairs but couldn't see anything beyond the first dozen or so steps, there was no glow from Jane's torch. Claustrophobia wrapped cold fingers around his throat and he took a deep breath, trying to calm himself. Where was she, why couldn't he see her light?

There was a noise to his right, like someone rubbing their hand on the wall. He leaned closer, seeing a smudge of shadow in the graffiti. Was that a hole in the plaster? He stepped back. Had someone plastered over a door?

He looked at the wall that faced the stairwell and tried to get his bearings. They'd walked across the Clicking room, with the back of the factory in sight and come through the door, meaning they were on the far side of the factory. The wall with the graffiti should have been the outside wall.

He tapped the facing wall with his knuckles and it sounded solid. He rapped the plaster in the middle of the graffiti and it sounded hollow. He tried both again and looked back up the stairs - had he somehow got his bearings wrong?

The rubbing sound came again and he leaned towards the graffiti, shining his torch on the hole. It was small, no bigger the half-moon on his little finger.

"Hello?" he said and rapped the wall again. Pressing his index finger against the hole, Paul felt the plaster give way under it. He stepped back, braced himself and kicked the wall over 'the'. The jarring impact threatened to knock him off balance but he stayed on his feet. Some fault lines were running off his target and he kicked at it again and again, then swapped feet. Within half a dozen kicks, he'd made a hole big enough to crawl through.

Jane looked at her watch. Paul had been gone for less than ten minutes, though it felt like longer.

The skin above her ankle had swollen, pushing her sock down, though the pain had eased slightly and her boot felt tight over the instep. She shifted position so her right leg was propped up by her left, elevation of the injury being about the only thing she could remember from her course. It meant she couldn't move much, so she sat and listened intently for sounds, especially any coming from the Clicking room. After the thump, she'd half expected someone to come through but no-one had.

Deciding she needed to check the extent of her injury, she hotched to the desk, grabbed the edge of it with her fingertips and pulled herself into a kneeling position. Slowly getting to her feet, putting all her weight on her left leg so her right foot could hover just above the floorboards, she carefully put her right leg down. The tip of her boot touched and there was no corresponding jab of pain. Gently, bracing herself on the desk, she put her foot down flat.

She relaxed her grip on the desk and her ankle roared. She quickly lifted it up. Putting her toe back down, she walked to the door and, although it was still painful, she could cope.

Sweating and tired, she sat in the same place as before. Limping wasn't brilliant, but it was better than not being able to walk at all and as soon as Paul got back, she wanted to make sure she could be right behind him.

Paul kicked away the last piece of plasterboard and then, slowly, put his hand into the gap. It went freely so, gingerly, he put his face in, wary for any sense of movement and ready to pull back at the first sign of it. Nothing happened. He pushed his head further through the hole and moved it carefully, panning his torch. He was looking onto a large landing he couldn't see the other side of. Steps led down to his left, more to his right led up.

Paul pushed his way through the plasterboard. The landing floor was lino, peeling at the edges with a lot of dark stains. The air smelled stale and metallic, with a sharp undercurrent of something rotten. He had no desire to find out what it was.

The left stairwell was narrow and there was graffiti on the walls but from his angle and with the light he couldn't make out what it was. Should he try that first and see if he could get out? If he could ring the police and get some help, that would help but would mean leaving Jane alone upstairs and Martin wherever he was. Could he do that? Should he?

He took a step down, his hand on the wall. It was damp and cold. He took another step and someone began to whisper behind him. He jerked his head around quickly, his pulse racing but what he could see of the landing was clear.

"Who's there? I can hear you!"

He could feel fear seeping through his body, stroking his scalp and filling his veins.

"I said I can hear you!"

He took another step and looked back. Was it the right thing to do? Jane wound him up, she always had, but she was injured and scared and leaving her alone wasn't the right thing to do.

"Shit," he said and went back up the stairs. The whispering was close by, still little more than a mumble. He didn't want to go onto the landing and tensed himself, taking a deep breath before the final step.

"You're not fucking funny," he said loudly as he moved, looking to his left and expecting to see someone. The landing was empty but the whispering continued, as if the person was right behind him.

"I know you're here," he said but didn't believe the words even as they left his mouth. He'd assumed, as the others probably had, it was kids - the one in the rough cutting room, the ones playing the choir recording, the whispering here. Just a bunch of youths with nothing better to do than scare the shit out of some adults who should have seen through it from the start.

But he could still hear the whispering and the only disturbance in the dust was by the hole in the wall and towards the stairwell. The landing had been deserted for some time.

Tom had been right.

Paul rushed across the landing and up the stairs, grabbing the banisters for support. He could still hear the whispering.

Jane gently touched the swelling above her right ankle. It hadn't got better or worse, which she supposed was a good thing, though whether she could make any kind of distance on it was another matter altogether.

She rubbed her neck and, for about the hundredth time, leaned forward to make sure the Clicking room door was still closed. She didn't believe in ghosts or the supernatural but she couldn't explain whatever she'd seen behind the desk and the thing crawling on the floor. And if someone was in there, why hadn't they come out? And the singing, what was that?

She sat back and took a deep breath. None of it mattered, of course, the only important thing was to find Martin and get help for Gwen, assuming Paul came back for her.

What if he didn't?

It was a silly thought, she knew that but couldn't seem to shake it - maybe it was the darkness, the fear, the pain or their crossed words beforehand. If he found a way out, would he not ring the police before he came back for her?

Maybe he'd found Martin and been so intent on making sure he was okay, he forgot about her.

Would Martin forget her?

She felt a cold chill run across her chest and looked into the landing again. Where was he? The darkness seemed to be gathering the way it had in the Clicking room and she didn't like it - the feeling of claustrophobia it engendered made worse by the lack of her mobility.

She felt the panic rising and tried to deep-breath it away then heard a faint squeak, the sound a trainer makes on tiles. Jane clasped a hand to her mouth to cover any sound and looked into the corridor, expecting to see Paul's torch beam but it was as dark as it had been.

Was her imagination playing tricks? She willed there to be another sound and time stretched, the only sounds the operation of her body. She'd just about convinced herself it was an aural hallucination when she heard the squeak again.

Leaning her head towards the door, she waited a bit longer, counting down in her head this time - one, two three.

Another squeak - could it be someone coming upstairs? Could it be him?

"Paul?" she said, not wanting to raise her voice too loudly. The only response was the squeak of him taking another step. Now she thought she could hear his breathing, quick and heavy as if he'd been running - had he seen something else? Was that why she couldn't see his torch beam, had he lost his hat somewhere downstairs?

Another step. The breathing, though slowing, seemed to get heavier. Something didn't feel right.

"Paul?"

The footsteps got louder, the breathing heavier with each exhalation. Was he taking the piss, trying to scare her?

The footsteps stopped and she heard grit crunch under soles. The breathing softened slightly as if he'd finally reached the top of the stairs.

"Paul, are you alright?"

Again there was no answer, just the breathing.

"This isn't funny you know," she said.

There was a clattering from the corner of the room and she shrieked, pushing herself further into her own corner. The hatch under the desk was opening. She tried to shriek again, realised she was holding her breath. Her chest ached.

"It's me, it's me," she heard Paul say, "you're okay."

The hatch was pushed fully up and she saw him, his torch beam scanning the room until he saw her. "I didn't mean to scare you but I found another stairwell and it came out here."

"But..." she said and looked towards the door. "You can't be there, I just heard someone come up the stairs breathing heavily. I thought it was you."

"Shit!" He scrambled through the hatch and rushed out the door. "There's nobody here."

"There has to be, I heard them come up."

"No." He came back into the office and squatted in front of her. "We need to get out of here."

With his help, she got to her feet but didn't let go of his arm when she was upright. He looked at her and raised his eyebrows.

"What's happening Paul?" She bit her lip, not wanting to acknowledge something was wrong but not able now to dismiss it either. "All of this, it's time you were straight with me."

"We have to go, Jane, come on, I'll help you through the hatch."

She pointed at his chest. "Something weird's going on in here and you know something about it."

"How could I?"

"All these things, the kid, the person I saw, the singing, someone coming upstairs. I thought it was a gang of kids but now I'm not so sure."

"That's what I thought too."

"Bullshit. What's going on Paul?" She looked at him, her light shining full in his face. He held up his hand but she didn't move her head. "Tell me the truth."

"I'll tell you but we need to get moving."

She nodded and he guided her to the hatch, holding her right arm as she hobbled, wincing every other step.

"Do you think it's broken?"

"I don't think so, but it's fucking painful to put any pressure on."

"Maybe a bad sprain?" he said. "If you sit on the edge, that'll probably be easier."

Jane held onto him and the edge of the desk, lowering herself to the floor. She looked into the hatch and saw a narrow staircase disappear into darkness. "How did you find this?"

"From the stairwell through there," he said. "It ended at a wall I had to kick in."

"And this goes all the way down?"

"It goes down, certainly. Let me go first though, in case you slip."

"I'm not going to slip," she said, an edge in her voice.

He was immediately apologetic. "I know, fully fit you wouldn't but you'll be limping."

She nodded. "Okay, but don't race off."
"I promise."

Chapter 13

The darkness was absolute.

Martin knew it wasn't going to get better - he was in a brick channel in the middle of a building with no outside access - but he'd hoped his eyes might adjust even slightly. They hadn't.

There was also the silence. Apart from the sounds of his body - his breath rattling in his throat, his pulse - there was nothing and it seemed to ring in his ears.

When he'd come to a skidding halt, the pain in his toes, legs, hands and arms had been so intense for a while he couldn't focus on anything other than it. But as it settled, the realisation of where he was descended like a wet suffocating blanket. Those first few moments had been the worst, as he fought to get enough air in his lungs, as he tried to angle his shoulders to move his chest so it wasn't pressing into the brick, to give himself enough space to suck in oxygen.

He could feel the panic attack coming, the tension growing in his shoulders, his stress-ache strong enough it wouldn't hurt more if he bashed his head against the roof of this too-fucking-narrow channel.

"Oh my God," he said, feeling his heart beat faster. He tried to take slower, deeper breaths but it was hard to do - he realised he was panting, the sound of it far too loud in the confined space and that scared him too. What if he got so frightened he had a heart attack? That thought just served to scare him more, speeding his breathing up further.

"No," he said, gasping. He closed his eyes, saw red streaks flash and breathed in through his nose. It wasn't quick enough, he wasn't filling his lungs and opened his mouth, coughing as he inhaled dust. The coughs hurt, pushing his back against the bricks and interfered with his breathing as well, setting off another panic.

He began to cry, heavy tears running down his cheeks. He felt his nose run, breathed in and his left nostril was blocked. He couldn't get enough breath, he coughed, more pain.

"Stop," he said, "stop it."

It didn't work. He gasped, his heartbeat increasing with his breathing and saw the red streaks again.

"Daddy? Daddy?"

Martin had just positioned the red toy phone in the lightbox to his satisfaction but Daisy sounded panicked. He opened the office door and went through to the kitchen. "What's up?" he called.

"I can't find Carla."

"Is she hiding?"

"Yes, we're playing hide and seek."

"Then I can't tell you where she is, you have to find her."

"But she's not anywhere."

With a sigh, Martin walked through the patio doors into the garden. Jenkins next door had already declared audio war on the girls and Frank Sinatra was singing "I Can't Stop Loving You" too loudly.

"Where are you?" he asked.

Daisy poked her head through the wendy house door. "Here, silly," she said.

"Have you looked for Carla?"

113

"Yes, all over the garden."

"Did she go into the house?"

"You told us not to."

"You're right." He heard a knocking sound and assumed it was Jenkins, knocking on the window to remind Martin as to why he'd felt the need to turn his stereo up so loud. Martin ignored it. "Have you checked everywhere out here?"

Their walled garden wasn't really big enough to hide in, even for a six-year-old but he dutifully checked behind the wheelie-bin and in the shed. "No," he said finally, "she's not here."

"I told you," said Daisy. She followed him around the garden and now stood with her hands on her hips, a stern expression inferring she felt he was wasting time.

"Well she must be in the house then."

The knocking came again and this time Martin looked up but there was nobody at either of the Jenkins rear windows. He moved his head, listening for the sound again. It seemed to be coming from his roof.

"Stay here," he said to Daisy and ran into the house, taking the stairs two at a time. On the landing, he saw the loft door was shut and realised how stupid his panic had been, how would she have even got up there.

"Okay," he called, "you can come out now Carla, you won."

"Daddy?" The voice was distant, muffled. "Daddy?"

"Yes?" he called.

"Help me, I'm stuck here and I can't get out."

"Where are you love?"

"I'm stuck and it's dark, please help me..."

Martin awoke with a start, banging his head against the

roof of the channel. His face felt sore, his nose slightly bunged up and he tried to keep his head up, assuming it was the angle causing him grief.

"Shit," he hissed.

Were his eyes open? He pressed them shut and opened them wide but the level of darkness didn't change. Was he only imagining he'd opened them wide? He flexed his fingers and stared at where he thought his hand was, concentrating hard. Could he see a faint outline? No, he couldn't.

Perhaps he could push himself backwards? He pressed his right hand against the channel, but his left was stuck under him, pinned by his thigh. Remnants of pins and needles buzzed lazily at his wrist and he could feel grit in the raw skin of his palms.

He pushed again with his right hand but didn't move, even after pressing his feet into the walls, his toe singing in pain. The movement made him breathe quicker and he tilted his head to the side, trying to suck in more oxygen.

"Calm," he said, "calm down."

It didn't help, he could feel his heart beat racing. More red flashes burst in front of his eyes. "Calm," he said, but talking interfered with his breathing and he gulped in air, which didn't fill his lungs.

He coughed, breathed in dust, coughed again. Panic coursed through him and he could barely think straight. He tilted his head up as far as he could, alternating breathing through his mouth and nose. The dust cleared and he relaxed slightly.

A skittering sound came from somewhere behind him but he couldn't gauge how far back because he didn't know how far he'd fallen. If he shouted, would anyone be able to hear back in that room? What if Jane and Paul had come looking for him?

"Jane!" His voice sounded tired and faded. "Paul!" He heard a snuffling sound he couldn't quite place. "Jane?"

He waited, for them to shout back, or for the skittering or snuffling, but only heard his too-fast breathing. He thought he saw something move but knew it was just his imagination.

"Jane!"

How could they know he was here? Even when they got out of the Clicking room, assuming they didn't head straight outside, why would they go up the corridor away from reception? And what if the impossible geometry he'd discovered put them off? What if they didn't press on as far as he had, what if they didn't see the X marked on the wall? After all, it had been mostly smudged away when he saw it the second time, maybe it was gone completely by now.

And - and and and - even if they did go further along the corridor, even if they did find the X, how would they find the door with the curious legend on it? Why would they bother to enter? Why would they look into the mouth of the beast and call his name?

Would he hear them?

"Jane!" He heard the snuffling again and it reminded him of something. "Are you there?"

Something slid on grit and he felt a shower of it against his legs. Was somebody coming down the tunnel after him? Fresh panic surged through him, catching his breath in his throat. What if they pushed him further? He wasn't going to get out like this, if he was wedged in even more then he definitely wouldn't be able to move, perhaps wouldn't even be able to take a deep enough breath properly.

He smelt something different, something slightly off like milk on the turn. Could he smell his own tears? The air suddenly felt soft and used and he wondered if he could suffocate here?

The snuffling came again and he made the connection - it reminded him of a kid in Clara's class, who rubbed his nose and sniffed when he got excited. Was that it, one of the children who'd pushed him was now lowering themselves down?

"Go away," he said.

The snuffling stopped.

"Leave me alone."

There was no sound.

Fresh tears fell and made a kaleidoscope against his eyes. It took him a moment to realise that shouldn't be and blinked the tears away. Something flickered ahead and he looked directly at it, the palest of yellow glows.

"Jane?" he called, though he couldn't work out how she could be ahead of him. Unless - and this was too hopeful to wish for - the opening of the channel was only a few feet ahead and they'd found the base of it. Could he really be that close to safety? "Are you there? Is anyone there?"

What followed wasn't the silence he'd expected but a babbling sound, like a vessel being filled with water - the sound of a hot summer afternoon as he ran the outside tap to fill the girls paddling pool. But how would he hear water?

The glow grew brighter. He held up his hand and, though they were still vague, could see the general shape of his fingers.

"Jane!" They'd somehow figured out where he was.

How far down the floors was he? It felt like he'd fallen for a while, could he be near the ground floor, perhaps into the basement?

The tunnel got brighter by the slimmest of margins. Could it be daylight? He had no concept of the time and couldn't see his watch. After a few moments, he could see the shimmer of light over the lip of the channel in front of him. His eyes smarted after being denied light for so long and he couldn't move his hand to rub them. He blinked fast and more tears ran down his cheeks.

The shimmer moved from one side of the channel to the other, getting brighter all the time, the babbling noise a soundtrack to it.

"Jane?" The light was suddenly too bright and he closed his eyes against it. "You're blinding me!"

He squinted and the glare was as if someone was shining the torch straight at him. It was moving closer, still shifting from side-to-side. The babbling was louder and he heard a knocking, like hard plastic hitting brickwork.

A hat, a bump cap like his - that would explain the light too. Somebody was coming up the channel, wearing a bump cap!

"Jane," he called, "I'm here, I'm stuck."

The babbling got louder and the air got cooler.

"How are you getting up that quickly?" He'd assumed the channel narrowed as it went, it didn't make sense for there to be a bottleneck midway down.

The light got brighter, moving too quickly for it to be on someone's head.

Unless the cap was coming towards him on whatever was making the babbling sound, especially if that was also cooling down the air.

"Fuck," he said and panic flared through him. He pushed his hand against the wall, desperate to find a fingerhold in the brickwork but there was none.

The light got closer, turning lazily, light reflecting onto the ceiling like a disco ball.

The channel was filling with water.

The cap was close enough to grab and he turned it back to face down the channel. It was gone, the light reflecting back off brown water that came towards him at speed. He pulled his arm back as far as he could and the water hit his hand, shocking him with its coldness. It moved up his arm and he forced his head back as far as he could, panic surging like an electric charge through him.

The water reached his shoulder, ran up his clavicle, lapped at his chin. The cold made him gasp. Some splashed into his mouth and he spat it out. The water was on his chin and he twisted his head, trying to get some space, knowing he wouldn't be able to.

"Jane!" he screamed.

The water ran into his mouth and covered his face. He held his breath, seeing stars, his lungs screaming.

He breathed in.

Chapter 14

Paul helped her off the ledge and led the way. Within a few steps, there was darkness behind her and the bobbing lights of their torch beams danced crazily around the too-narrow stairwell. Jane put one hand on his shoulder, the other on the banister.

"So tell me," she reminded him.

"It was Tom," he said after a few moments. "He was interested in this place when we were at Gaffney Tech but couldn't get in. He talked about it a lot over the years and I thought it was just because he loved the place and wanted to explore it."

"And it wasn't?"

"No. You remember Gwen said her granddad told her stories?"

"Ghost stories, you mean?" she said slowly. She looked behind her, suddenly panicked, half expecting to see someone.

"Yeah. He'd done some research on the place and met a woman in Birmingham who was big into parapsychology and liked to explore haunted places. They went into old hospitals and mental asylums, anywhere there was some trace of supernatural activity."

Even though she was scared and had already made the mental leap from it being a gang of kids to something else altogether, she still felt a chill. "Really?"

"Yes. They'd go in, armed with cameras and all kinds of equipment and observe."

"And did they ever see anything?"

"Apparently. He sent me an email once saying they'd been on an expo and he was surprised his hair hadn't turned white."

"I didn't know that."

"Why would you? If we weren't here, having experienced this, would you have believed him?"

"No."

"But you would now."

"I might."

"Well he believed and started talking about this place again since he'd heard more through this woman's group."

The stairwell got wider and Paul moved over so that they could walk side-by-side. She let go of his shoulder and held his left hand instead, her left on the banister.

"I told you," he said, "it's just a normal stairwell now, running parallel with the one outside the office."

"But why would stairs go up into a narrow channel like that and then a hatch?"

He shrugged. "Maybe it was a common design in Victorian England."

"I can't see that somehow. So what did Tom hear about this place?"

"People saying things, like Gwen's granddad hearing noises or voices, things going bump in the night, the usual stuff. Then he researched Pocock and the history of the building. Tom reckons he disappeared sometime in the early 1900s and it was reported as his dying, with a burial and all else."

"Disappeared?"

"Vanished."

"Rubbish."

"Tom did the research, building on what others had

done and apparently Pocock was a really nasty piece of work. Most factories back then used child labour but he liked to beat them if they didn't work hard enough. And worse, if they didn't meet up to his standards or got on his nerves, he would kill them and bury the bodies in the basement."

"What? How would they cover that kind of thing up?"

He looked at her. "From over a hundred years ago? Good God, Jane, he could have said black was white and people would have believed him. And if the kids died of natural causes - and there were lots of those back then - they'd get buried in the basement too."

"You're making this up."

"I wish I was, Tom sent me all the documentation and I read through it over and over again."

"I don't believe it."

"The factory was kept up by his son, who wasn't the monster his father was but he was greedy and kept the child labour. His granddaughter inherited it and ran it, which is when Gwen's granddad would have been about and when they went out of business, she gave strict instructions that nobody was to sell the building or go into it."

"Like she knew the history and didn't want it found out?"

"Could be," he said. "As soon as she died, her family sold the place immediately."

"And now it's going to be flats."

"If they keep the shell and renovate, nobody will ever know but if they knock it down, the basement will be discovered along with any graves that might be there."

"Is why Tom came back?"

"He wanted to scout the place out, before he got the rest of his team in to check it out."

"So are you telling me this place is haunted?"

"You said it yourself."

"No Paul, I'm living in the real world and trying to make sense of everything that's happened."

"But you're thinking it."

"What else should I think?"

"It's what Tom thought."

"But he never made it, did he?" They walked in silence for a moment or two. "So if you knew all this, why the fuck did you ask us to come in here?"

"Because I thought it'd be a good legacy for Tom, if we did experience something and because I never expected anything to happen."

"And now we might've lost Gwen and have no idea where Martin is."

"I don't know what to say."

"How about that you're a twat?"

They came to the landing and he pointed. "You can't see it, but the staircase is over there."

"Where did you kick in the wall?"

"Over there. Come on, the quicker we move, the quicker…"

Someone whispered to her left and she turned, startled. "Did you hear that whispering?"

"No, but I did when I was here before."

"Who is it? Where are they?" She raised her voice. "Who's there?"

"It's nobody," said Paul.

"Rubbish," she said and left go of his hand, following the wall to the corner. She turned and walked the length of the landing, her left hand brushing plaster wall, moving her head from side to side though she didn't see anyone.

There was a dark space on the wall ahead and as she got closer, she could see rough edges. "I found your hole," she said but he didn't reply. When she turned around, she couldn't see his torch either. "Paul?"

The whispering got louder, coming from beside and behind her, the words a jumble she couldn't decipher. She made her way back, keeping her right hand against the wall.

Paul watched as Jane's torch beam dimmed and was finally swallowed by the gloom. Once again he felt the darkness press against him, tightening his chest and making it difficult to breathe.

"Jane?" he called. "Don't move too far away."

She didn't respond so he followed her trail, tracing his left hand along the wall to the corner. Her footprints in the dust ended just before the hole.

"Jane?"

Paul stood in front of the hole.

"Where did you go?" she demanded. "Why didn't you answer me?"

He looked startled to see her. "I couldn't see or hear you, where did you go?"

"I was right here." He grabbed for her hand and she gratefully took it. "I'm scared," she said.

"Me too, it seems like whatever it is about this place is stronger here."

"Can you hear the whispering?"

"No." He guided her to the top of the stairs. "This set is narrow too, I'll go first and you stick close behind."

They walked down the stairs in silence, though Jane could hear the faint hiss of whispering from the landing. She held onto the banister on either side and kept her torch beam focussed on the treads, making sure there were no gaps or holes in them. They went further than she thought they would, as if the staircase was double normal length and soon the banister felt damp.

"How far down does this go?" she asked finally.

Paul stopped and touched the wall. "It's wet," he said. "So's the banister."

He tried it and nodded. "The air smells damp too."

They walked down further until he said "there's another landing."

She tried to peer over his shoulder but couldn't see properly. The air was chilly now and she shivered. "Are there more stairs?"

"No, a door."

"Let's hope it's reception."

"We must be right at the edge of the factory now, so it might be an office or something."

Paul reached the bottom of the stairs and stepped to one side, so she could stand beside him. It wasn't a landing, more of an ante-room and she looked at the dark, blank walls with dismay. There was a single door across from them, which had metal braces over it and a large handle. He twisted it and pushed. The door swung open slowly, making a lot of noise as the rusted hinges groaned in movement. Beyond, she could see bare stone floor and not much else.

"Where the fuck are we?" she asked.

"I don't know but unless we want to go back upstairs, which I'd don't, we've got to go on."

"Let's go."

He nodded and, cautiously, went through the door. Jane followed him into a narrow corridor with grey, mould-spotted walls. The air was stale and dank.

"What is this?" she asked.

He just shook his head. The corridor turned to the right and they followed it. A few paces along there was a door in the wall on the left.

"Shall we?" he asked quietly.

"It could be reception," she whispered back. She hadn't intended to whisper but his quiet question and the claustrophobic feel of the corridor made her not want to make much noise, worried the echo might turn on them.

The door handle didn't turn so Paul moved on. Jane tried it herself as she passed but it wouldn't budge. There was another door a few more paces away, the handle equally stuck.

"What if we can't get out?" she asked.

"Then we just head back."

The third door was recessed slightly and there were silver and red streaks of paint on it. Paul tried the handle and it opened.

"Shall we go in?"

"Yeah, I need to get out of this corridor."

He went into the room, Jane right behind him and she looked around, her torch beam reflecting at her from the side wall. She couldn't make out any other details apart from the blank floorboards.

"Offices?" he asked.

"Maybe."

He started towards them, his torch beam focussed on the floor. The boards were dark and solid. The wall to her left was bare plaster. She couldn't see the other side of the room.

The reflections came from windows. "Three offices," he said.

"So what's this room?"

"Who knows?"

He opened the first door onto a small square room with no furniture or markings on the wall. The second office was the same.

"This is a waste of time," he said bitterly. "We need to find the main door."

Whispers filled the air and she touched his arm. There were more voices, the words unintelligible. Jane found it hard to breathe, the darkness billowing in front of her, caressing her cheeks and brushing lightly over her nose and mouth, a lovers embrace. Were their torch beams weakening? That thought scared her more than anything else had so far - she didn't have a problem with the dark or being closed in but there was something about this room, the dampness and the feeling of size, that made her feel closed in. She gasped in a breath, held it and tried to blow it out evenly.

"Are you alright?"

"No, I think I'm going to hyperventilate."

The singing began again, as loud as it had been in the Clicking room, though a different song this time, one she'd never heard before.

Old father Long-Legs
Can't say his prayers:
Take him by the left leg,
And throw him down the stairs.
And when he's at the bottom,
Before he long has lain,
Take him by the right leg,

And throw him up again.

The voices were spread in front of them. Tears ran down her cheeks. "Paul," she hissed, "what's happening?"

"I don't know," he said, panicked.

"I'm so scared."

He reached for her hand and she yelped, then grabbed it, squeezing it tight. "Don't leave me."

The choir got louder, singing as if enjoying themselves. Jane backed away, pulling Paul with her, her free hand reaching for the second office doorway. They kept their torches trained straight ahead but could see nothing in the gloom.

"What are you doing here?"

The voice of the angry man was so loud it startled Jane and she looked to her right, where it had come from. "Get back to your bunks you dirty little arabs, afore I thrash you to Kingdom come."

The singing stopped and there was movement around them. Something tugged at her arm and leg, she felt air move as people passed her. She screamed and Paul gripped her hand tighter.

"I can feel it," he said.

More movement, a shout and a loud slap. A child began to cry, more called out. "You little guttersnipes, never satisfied. Well, I'll give you something to cry about."

There was a whistling sound, like a belt being whipped and another child cried out. Something hit Jane's side and knocked her into Paul, but he managed to maintain his balance. She felt small hands on her back, belly and legs.

"What'll we do with you then?" asked the angry man, still invisible but very close. "Shall I tan you until the blood seeps out?"

A child screamed. Another yelled.

"Come on," said Paul and he turned, stumbled and dragged her towards the second office. Things were in her way that she couldn't see and her sweaty fingers slid through Paul's.

"Come back!" she shouted and he turned, reaching out his hand, borne away by blurs in the darkness.

His torch beam disappeared and, with it, the noise from the room.

Jane dropped to her knees, wincing at the pain in her ankle.

The silence was too much, her torch beam not enough to penetrate the darkness and she felt a suffocating claustrophobia settle over her. She tried to keep her breathing regular and bit her lip hard, to shake herself up. She couldn't succumb to this, she needed to find Paul or, failing that, get out into that horrible, awful, corridor.

It was too much, too oppressive for her to even think clearly.

When a small voice next to her said "where's my Mummy?" she only had the energy to scream.

Chapter 15

Paul was buffeted into the second office and grabbed for the door frame as he was pushed past it. His fingers closed on air and he went into the room, struggling to stay on his feet.

He hit the back wall hard, the wind knocking out of him and he leaned forward, trying to catch his breath. The singing began, quieter now, accompanied by squeals and giggles. He sensed, rather than felt, movement and the office seemed to shift and then he was in another room, the floor beneath him stopping suddenly, the momentum almost pushing him sideways.

The torch beam cut a shaft through a misty atmosphere that hung in front of the darkness. There were flashes of reflection, as if catching the opposite wall but he couldn't tell how far away it was.

He looked at the disc he was standing on, blackness below that. To this left and right, there was a brick lip perhaps eight inches wide.

"Fuck," he said, putting his arms against the slick wall behind him. Where the hell was he? The air was heavy, damp and cold and he could hear steady dripping from somewhere in the darkness. He pressed his knees back until they came into contact with the wall, suddenly afraid his sense of balance would let him down. He felt cold, pins and needles in his fingertips as they twitched. He daren't move, he couldn't. It might only be a few feet to the floor but it might be twenty or thirty and the unknown terrified him.

How long could he stand like this, before his muscles cramped? Apart from the Glue Club, nobody knew they were in here so the chance of rescue was non-existent.

"Jane?" His voice echoed back, mockingly. "Are you there?"

His mouth was dry and he couldn't swallow properly. He tilted his head back as far as he could, his torch pointing towards a ceiling he couldn't see. How far up could this room go? Surely it had to be the ground floor, if not the basement level. They wouldn't have dug enough of a pit that his torch couldn't search out details. He looked towards the wall on the other side of the room. The mist shifted slightly, the light reflecting off a slick, stone surface. It didn't look to be that far away, perhaps fifteen feet, but that must have been a trick of the light, it was too ridiculously narrow.

Something made a scrabbling sound below.

Heartbeat thudding, his throat clicking around the words, he called "Is anybody there?"

"Anybody there?" echoed back.

And, below that, a small voice said "just us."

He breathed in sharply, the pins and needles running up his arms. He closed his eyes, tears squeezing onto his cheeks and got the sensation he was swaying forward. His eyes snapped open but he couldn't tell if he was moving or not, so pressed himself back hard against the wall. His splayed fingers grasped for purchase but found none.

The scrabbling came again and he felt more tears on his cheeks.

"Help!" he shouted, more to distract himself than anything but the sound brought activity that seemed to be all around him. His voice sounded too high, fractured.

"Don't panic," he shouted and felt a laugh bubble in his chest. That would be even worse than panicking, if he got a sudden touch of the hysterics. Any movement and he'd be off this ledge.

There was a warm sensation in his quads, just above his knees. He tried not to think about it.

"Focus," he said, willing himself to take deep breaths. There had to be a way out of this, he couldn't give in now.

Hands pressed against his left leg and he screamed. He looked down and felt his centre of balance shift. Trying to push himself backwards, his fingertips raked the wall for anything to grab hold of but there was nothing. Dropping further forward, he tried to angle his body to the side - maybe, if he fell, he could twist and grab hold of the ledge. Would that work?

Further forward, the torch beam cutting through the darkness. A quick blur in front of him, as if his torch light was reflected back by eyes and then he was pitching over, his arms flailing and he screamed as he fell.

The stone floor was cold and damp.

Paul came to with a gasp, opening his eyes to darkness, his back and belly full of pain that made him cry out. He shifted his right elbow and felt a stabbing pain in his side. His legs wouldn't move and pain spiked his lower back. Had he broken something, his back maybe, in the fall?

"Shit," he said, the word petering out, the effort to say it almost too much.

He was on his right side and looking at two sources of light, one close enough to touch, the other some way away. Both were pointing towards him, making it difficult to see anything else.

The scrabbling noise was nearer now. Ignoring it, he reached for the bump cap, catching the peak with his fingers and pulled it towards him. Lifting it slightly, he aimed it towards his side and glanced down. At first, what he was looking at didn't make any sense and he wondered if he was concussed too. He blinked, as if that would help and looked again. The metal spike was still there, poking through his jacket, the point of it dark with blood and matter.

Bile rose in his throat.

It had to be a mistake. Shutting out the pain in his ribs and lower back as best he could, he tried to shift his torso but it wouldn't move. He put the cap on the floor and slid his left hand down his back. There was a puddle of a cold, thick liquid he knew was blood before he lifted his hand and saw it dripping from his fingers.

"Shit," he said, a sob catching in his throat.

He slid his hand back across the slick stone. The spike came out of the ground under his ribs. There was a thread on it and three or four fingers width before it disappeared into his jacket.

Paul managed to turn his head slightly, the movement pushing heat through this belly, before he was sick. A heavy thumping pulse started behind his eyes and his breathing got quicker. He tried to keep still, willing himself to think, but his thoughts were racing.

"Calm," he said. It hurt to take a breath and he was having trouble focussing. "Calm."

His throat felt dry and he wanted to close his eyes but forced them open. Now wasn't the time to sleep.

Being as careful as he could, he turned the bump cap toward the other light. It was on the floor in front of a narrow slit in the wall, which had water running out of it. He couldn't see any sign of his friends. Between him and the hole in the wall he could see half a dozen thick metal rings set into the floor. Some of them had small piles of rags next to them.

The scrabbling sound came from close behind him.

"What are you waiting for?" he gasped, hoping to hear that little voice again but there was no reply. Instead, he heard metal shriek against metal, somewhere to his right. There was a heavy clang and the noise of something being lifted, perhaps a drain cover. The sound of rushing water filled the room and, a few moments later, he felt it on his face. It smelled terrible, stagnant and rotten and he moved his head as the water caressed his cheek.

"You need to be taught a lesson!" someone roared and the sound made him jump, pulling him against the spike and making him cry out. Scared that the angry person might come to him, he bit his lip hard enough to taste blood.

Children cried and begged, their words caught in a blur of sobbing.

"You're too slow for me and too expensive to feed." More metal clanged against metal. "I'll pin you down," the man growled, "and give you a bath."

There was more sobbing as the water level rose, forcing Paul to lift his head. His neck pinged with pain.

"Don't fret little ones," the voice said and laughed, "you won't be cold for long."

The small bundles of rags moved with the water and as they did Paul saw the stark whiteness of bone hidden within them. The rags moved, eddying but didn't float for long as the chains attached them to the metal rings were revealed.

The water splashed his face and he swallowed some, spitting it out straight away though the taste lingered.

"Sleep well, little ones," said the voice and then all Paul could hear, above his own laboured breathing, was sobbing and the splash of water.

Chapter 16

There was only silence.

Jane opened her eyes and looked around slowly but there was no sign of Paul. Getting to her feet, she checked the offices but he wasn't there either.

She leaned against the wall, a heavy hot sensation in her belly. She was alone and tried to fight back the feelings of fear and panic she could already feel running through her. Thoughts flashed into her mind, of Brian and her house, of her work and driving down the M1, of summer evenings sitting in the garden enjoying a glass of wine and listening to the radio.

"No," she said, needing to hear something in the stillness.

The darkness was deeper than before, heavier almost, a thick weight that threatened to swamp her with its cool embrace. She could feel her breath coming in quick gasps, her lungs not capable of inhaling enough oxygen to keep her going.

She hobbled to the door, her ankle barking with pain every time she put weight on it and leaned against the jamb. The corridor, which now seemed even narrower than before, swam in her vision and she let her head drop, closing her eyes.

"Keep it together," she said. Fainting now was not a good idea but neither was stopping and letting the fears consume her.

"Go," she said.

She turned left, simply because right led back up

those stairs and with her hands on either wall and her head down to light the way, she hobbled down the corridor, listening to her ragged breathing and the unsteady tattoo of her shoes on the stone floor. The walls got damper, slicker but she kept moving, not wanting to break the momentum.

Voices began behind her.

Jane slowed a little, glancing back quickly but kept going.

The voices got louder, children talking excitedly.

"Where are you going?" demanded a loud and angry voice.

Jane, her shoulders pinching in coldness, tried to ignore the voice. It wasn't talking to her, it couldn't be. She needed to keep going, to ignore this madness.

"Come back here, you little arabs, I'll teach you some manners."

The children's voices rose in pitch. There was a crack, like leather whipping flesh and she heard a grunting cry of pain. More children yelled and there was another crack.

She could feel them now, almost upon her and tried to speed up but it was impossible to put her foot down properly.

"Stand still!"

The voice, aggressive and mean, filled her head and made her cry.

Another crack and she felt the whisper of it against her back. The clamour of the children was so close now she thought she could smell their sweat and fear.

She stumbled, her right leg slipping on a patch of water and fell to the side. She hit the wall and slid forward, then pushed herself up into a sitting position, pulling her knees to her chest and covering her head with her arms.

She felt the swarm of children pass her, then the heavy tread of the pursuing man.

After he went by, she dared to peek, dropping her arms as she stared into the narrow stone walled room she was sitting across from. The wet cobbled floor, studded with metal rings, reflected the light of the gas lamps on the walls. Across the room was a small podium, a hatch wheel on top of it.

The children rushed towards it, careful to step over the small bundles of rags that were next to the metal rings. The man, wearing tweeds and high boots, raced after them, holding a riding crop above his head.

The first of the children reached the podium and four faced back, creating a wall around one who turned the hatch wheel. Water ran over the podium as the child pushed up a wide, circular drain cover.

The man closed the gap, whipped at a child but missed. He slipped, staggered and fell against another child, knocking them both to the floor. The child was out from under him in a flash and more piled on top of the man, beating him with their tiny fists and kicking him. The man got to his feet with a growl, throwing a couple of the children against the far wall.

"You need to be taught a lesson!" he roared and Jane flinched at the venom in his voice.

There was more squealing from the children and she could hear sobbing now. Even the ones on the podium had stopped and faced him, heads down.

"I'll pin you down and give you a bath," he said, whipping at another child who cried out.

Then they moved, almost as one, some grabbing his

legs, some pushing him from behind. The sudden movement took him by surprise and he lost his balance, going down to his right. The children let go and his head clattered against the podium, then they grabbed anything they could and pushed him onto the platform.

The man yelled, his voice wavering. The children pushed him forwards and he disappeared with a loud splash. One of the children jumped up and pulled down the drain cover, spinning the wheel quickly.

A couple of the children cheered.

Jane sat forward, favouring her ankle. She could hear the man hitting the drain cover. The children laughed, jumping on it and singing a song.

"Where's my mummy?"

The voice was right beside her and she screamed. Leaning forward, she got to her feet, her ankle threatening to give way, pain racing up and down her leg. She braced her hand against her knee, hobbling towards the doorway which was now dark. She could hear singing but it didn't cover the pounding of fists against metal.

In the doorway, the dank smell of dirty water assailed her and she gagged.

"Mummy?"

She looked both ways but there was nobody else in the corridor. She took a step into the darkness of the room and there was nothing under her foot. She grabbed for the jamb, her fingers glancing against the woodwork but she couldn't get a grip. Her left leg hung in space, over-balancing her and she tried to throw herself sideways but gravity was already pulling her the other way.

Jane didn't fall far, landing on her side on soft earth that smelled damp and rich. Her bump cap fell away, sliding just out of her reach. Groaning, she rolled onto her back, the torch to her left, shining in her eyes.

She felt small vibrations in the floor and looked to the right. The torch cast her shadow against the far wall. Ahead of her, the ground seemed to be shaking, the soft earth moving and casting motes into the light.

Something pushed up from under the floor. It took her a moment to realise it was a small hand. There was more movement but she couldn't take it in, could feel the shock closing her down as the horror washed over her.

More hands struggling as the long-dead corpses pushed out of the soft earth of their graves.

She screamed.

Still, they came.

"Mummy....?"

Author Notes & Bio

Peter Mark May & I go back a long way and, at the WFC Con in Brighton in 2013, he asked if I'd like to write a novella for Hersham Horror Books. I happily agreed but life (and health) got in the way and even though we chatted about it on occasion, time seemed to slip away from me. Then, in 2015, he asked again and the timing was right and things just clicked.

I'd been working on an idea for a short story for an anthology that, on reflection, was never going to happen but the core of it - a group of friends who are urban explorers investigating an old factory in the middle that was due for demolition - wouldn't leave me. I worked on it a bit more, found a single image - graves in the basement - and that was it. I pitched the idea to Pete, he liked it and I was off.

My main goal was to make it a proper horror novella. My novella Drive had shown me a different path (which I explored with my novelette Polly, to be released later this year) and I thought it'd be nice to write an old-school shocker before I looked towards dark thrillers.

Pocock's is fictitious but the location is the Victorian part of a plastics factory in Rothwell I pass on my daily walks and I used its outside appearance and windows (and added a canal to Gaffney too). The number of old friends was determined by the number of deaths I wanted to stage (most of them dreamed up as I chatted with my

141

old friend David Roberts as we had Christmas dinner) and it took me a while to realise they were meeting up because one of their group had just died. The characters themselves were in flux for a long time as I tried to ally them to real people before going the other way and building them up based on their relationships with the GLUE club. Having said that, Jane became an auditor because we had them in the office as I was making notes a baker and Martin was a photographer because I'd just read something online about building your own light box.

I found some books on the Northants boot and shoe industry, one of which showed a typical layout - I stole it, shamelessly. Otherwise, there was no research at all - the factory was a blank canvas and I made it do as I wanted.

With the writing itself, I found I struggled when all four characters were "on stage" at the same time, as I tried to give all of them enough dialogue to justify them being there and it became much easier when they were separated. For chapters 2 - 5 I adopted a method my friend, the sci-fi writer Ian Whates, uses and had them all open on one file, so I could dot backwards and forwards as I built the story and the characters. Similarly, when Martin and Paul & Jane get separated, I wrote their pieces as one (I did Martin first, found the cliff-hanger and then wrote the chapter where he suffers terribly with claustrophobia, which was quite uncomfortable).

Bio:

Mark West was born in Northamptonshire in 1969 and now lives there with his wife Alison and their young son Matthew. Since discovering the small press in 1998 he has published over ninety short stories, two novels (*In The Rain With The Dead* and *Conjure*), a novelette (**The Mill**), a chapbook (*What Gets Left Behind*), a collection (*Strange Tales*) and two novellas (*Drive*, which was nominated for a British Fantasy Society Award and *The Lost Film*). He has more short stories and novellas forthcoming and he is currently working on a novel.

Away from writing, he enjoys reading, walking, cycling, watching films and playing Dudeball with his son.

He can be contacted through his website at www.markwest.org.uk and is also on Twitter as @MarkEWest

Mark West

Fogbound From 5, Alt-Dead, Alt-Zombie. Siblings, Anatomy of
Death, Demons & Devilry and Dead Water. The Curse of the
Mummy; Wolf, Ghost, Zombie, Monster & Vampire.

Hersham Horror Books

http://silenthater.wix.com/hersham-horror-books#

Proof

Made in the USA
Charleston, SC
14 August 2016